Keep the Faith

# clearwater crossing

# Keep the Faith

## laura peyton roberts

BANTAM BOOKS
NEW YORK • TORONTO • LONDON • SYDNEY • AUCKLAND

RL 5.8, age 12 and up
KEEP THE FAITH
A Bantam Book / December 1998

ISBN 0-553-49259-4

Published simultaneously in the United States and Canada.

Bantam Books are published by Bantam Books, a division of Bantam
Doubleday Dell Publishing Group, Inc. Its trademark, consisting of the
words "Bantam Books" and the portrayal of a rooster, is Registered in
U.S. Patent and Trademark Office and in other countries. Marca Reg-
istrada. Bantam Books, 1540 Broadway, New York, New York 10036.

PRINTED IN THE UNITED STATES OF AMERICA

CWO    10   9   8   7   6   5   4   3

*For Renee.*
*Keep the faith.*

*Now faith is being sure of what we hope for and certain of what we do not see.*

*Hebrews 11:1*

# One

Miguel del Rios wheeled around as if he'd been shot in the back.

"What?" he shouted. He'd heard his sister—half the neighborhood must have heard her. He just wanted to hear those incredible words again.

"The kidney! The kidney!" Rosa cried excitedly. "They've got it! Oh, Miguel . . . *hurry!*"

Leaving Leah Rosenthal crying in the middle of his front walkway, he ran back into his house. He didn't think about the fact that he'd been in the middle of breaking up with her. Under the circumstances, he barely thought of her at all. The only thing on his mind was getting to his mother.

He burst through the front door and found her sitting at the dinette, tears of joy sliding down her cheeks. Her gray-streaked hair was pulled back into its usual neat bun, but the wadded tissue in her shaking hands betrayed her emotions. "Oh, Miguel!" she said. "Our prayers have been answered. I'm so happy."

*Our* prayers. The words hit him hard. He had prayed for this too.

Rosa moved behind their mother and put impatient hands on her shoulders. "Mom, we ought to be leaving for the hospital. Dr. Gibbons said to come right away."

"Where's your suitcase?" Miguel asked, even though he knew it was packed and under his mother's bed, just as it had been since the day she went on the kidney recipient waiting list. "You should be getting ready."

"I am ready. I just want to sit here and thank God a minute and pray for the donor's family."

Miguel hung his head. He'd been so busy thinking of himself that he hadn't yet stopped to consider that the kidney his mother would receive had belonged to someone who'd just died. Miguel might never know who or how—but wherever that person's family was gathered, there was bound to be terrible grief. He hesitated a moment, watching his mother pray, before he went silently off to the bedroom she shared with Rosa.

Under Mrs. del Rios's bed, the small overnight case she had packed long ago lay in the darkness against the wall. He reached to pull it out and brushed away a few dust bunnies. Once a kidney was harvested, there was a window of only about fifteen hours before it had to be placed in its new body. In that little amount of time, the doctors had

2

to do tissue matching to decide who the most suitable recipient was, contact that person and get him or her to the hospital, perform a physical examination and draw blood for final cross-matching, and prepare the patient for a surgery that usually took four to five hours. They might have to do dialysis, too, before the surgery could proceed. This was why the del Rioses had to hurry, why the operation would take place that very night. This was why his mother hadn't been away from a phone for longer than fifteen minutes in the last two years, why her suitcase was already packed. . . .

Miguel felt tears start down his cheeks. He wiped them distractedly as he hurried to the bathroom to get his mother's toothbrush. He didn't even know why he was crying. It could have been either happiness for his mother or sadness for the person who had died. It could have been relief, such sweet relief after the agony of waiting.

Or it could have been fear. Fear that, after all this time, this was only a false alarm, that something would be wrong either with the kidney or with his mother's health that would prevent the surgery from going forward. Fear that it wouldn't go well. Fear of a million undefined possibilities that preyed on the edges of his mind, making his lungs feel too small for the way he was breathing as he rushed back to put the toothbrush in his mother's bag.

Mrs. del Rios walked in as he was zipping it up.

She looked calmer now, in control again. Rosa bounced along behind her, her cheeks flushed pink and her brown eyes full of excitement.

"I got your toothbrush," he said.

"Thanks. Did you get my hairbrush, too?"

Miguel hadn't thought of that. He started in the direction of the bathroom, but Rosa headed him off.

"I'll get it! Go warm up the car, Miguel."

"Good idea, *mi vida*." Mrs. del Rios unzipped the case Miguel had zipped a moment before. "I just want to make sure I have everything. I'll be there in a minute."

Miguel paused only long enough to grab his leather bomber jacket before he ran outside into the cold early evening. His car was parked in front, under the streetlight. Letting himself in, he cranked the key in the ignition, watching in the rearview mirror as hot air chugged from the tailpipe and made a cloud of vapor behind him.

When he looked forward again, he noticed that Leah's car was gone from the other side of the street, but the fact didn't really register. Instead, he closed his eyes and prayed: *Please, God, let this go well. Please, let it go well. Please, God.* He said it over and over again, as if repetition were all that mattered.

The door yanked open on the curb side, jolting Miguel back to the present. Rosa climbed into the backseat, his mother took the front, and, almost before he knew it, Miguel was pulling away from the curb, steering the noisy old car down the quiet street. It felt like a dream, like functioning underwater. His senses were dull and heavy, barely able to take in Rosa's nervous chatter or his mother's reassurances.

Suddenly they were parking at the hospital, checking in, being greeted by Dr. Gibbons on the fourth floor—everything was a blur. An instant later his mom was hustled off for blood tests and surgery preparation, and he and Rosa were left behind in the waiting room.

"I'll come find you before she goes into the O.R.," Dr. Gibbons promised over her shoulder as she shepherded their mother off. "You'll get to see her before the surgery."

Mrs. del Rios turned and waved calmly. "I love you. Be good," she mouthed. She turned the corner and was gone.

"Now what?" Miguel groaned, sinking into a lobby chair.

Rosa shrugged. "Now we wait." Considering she was two years younger than he was—fifteen to his seventeen—she was taking things pretty well. Better than he was—he felt sure of that. His stomach was flopping like a fish out of water, while the muscles in his neck and shoulders had become so tight that his head was pounding.

Waiting for Dr. Gibbons to come back was agony.

5

An hour ticked by. Two. They felt longer than the two years the family had waited for the kidney in the first place. Rosa flipped through stale waiting-room magazines, occasionally reading something, but Miguel's agitation was barely in check. He paced—from the chair to the reception counter to the vending machines to the chair, where he'd sit down only to pop up again a minute later. *Please, God, let this go well. Let her get well. Please, God,* he prayed fervently as he walked, each stop on his circuit like a bead on a rosary.

Miguel glanced at the small, square window at the end of the hall. Full darkness had fallen outside. *Why is this taking so long?* he worried. *What are they doing?*

He wished Leah were there. No, wait—he was mad at Leah. His eyes squeezed shut against the pain of the added burden. Of all the times to break up, why did it have to be now, when he needed her most?

*Because she betrayed you, that's why.* But somehow he couldn't muster the anger he knew he ought to feel. Not with his mom about to be cut open any second. He'd think about Leah later, he decided, when his mom was safe and resting. He was sure he'd be plenty angry with Leah then.

At last Dr. Gibbons reappeared, her wiry orange hair escaping her bushy ponytail. "Okay! Everything looks great. We've got your mom all prepped and in a room, and we're just about ready to go. We

6

gave her something to make her sleepy, but you can come wish her luck before she goes into surgery."

*Luck!* Miguel's alarm must have been all over his face.

"It's just an expression," Dr. Gibbons reassured him. "Everything's looking very good. Very positive."

He followed the doctor and Rosa to his mother's room. Mrs. del Rios was lying in a bed with bars on the sides, wearing a hospital gown. Her eyes were half closed, her head propped on a pillow. She looked so frail and helpless, it almost broke his heart.

"Are you all right?" he demanded, rushing to her side.

"Fine. Fine, *mi vida*," she murmured.

"What took so long?" Rosa asked.

"We had to do one last dialysis," Dr. Gibbons answered for her.

The words "one last dialysis" brought a smile to Mrs. del Rios's lips. "You don't know how good that sounds."

A pair of orderlies came into the room with a gurney, ready to take her to the operating room.

"Okay! Well, I'll see the two of you in about four hours," Dr. Gibbons told Miguel and Rosa. "Keep the faith." She smiled down at Mrs. del Rios. "And I'll see *you* in a few minutes." The orderlies moved forward to transfer Mrs. del Rios onto the gurney, and Dr. Gibbons left the room.

"Are you scared?" Rosa whispered to her mother.

"A little," she admitted with a rueful smile. "But I shouldn't be. I know God's here with me." She reached for both her children's hands and squeezed them hard. "See you soon."

The orderlies wheeled her from the room a moment later. Miguel sank into a chair, gripping his aching head in his hands.

"It's going to be okay, Miguel," said Rosa, taking the seat beside him.

"How do you know? You're not a doctor."

"No, but the doctor just told you the same thing."

"She did not! She said to keep the faith."

Rosa smiled. "It's good advice. You ought to take it."

"What's that supposed to mean? You think I'm not praying for Mom?"

"Faith isn't only praying, Miguel. The Bible says faith is being certain of what you do not see."

Miguel stared at her blankly. He was having a nervous breakdown and she was quoting him scripture? What was wrong with her?

"Of course, prayer's good too." She stood up and shoved her hands into the pockets of her faded jeans. "I'm going to go get a Coke. Want anything?"

"What?" he said irritably. "No."

She held out an empty palm. "Got any quarters?"

He gave her his change in a daze, barely noticing when she left. His mother had been assigned to a double room, but there was no one in the other bed. Miguel was alone.

" 'Keep the faith,' " he repeated disgustedly. First he had to *have* some faith. And why was a doctor saying that, anyway? It didn't exactly inspire confidence. Dr. Gibbons was so young, she probably didn't know any better.

"Oh, God," he groaned, dropping his head back into his hands at the thought.

He remembered the night a couple of weeks before when he'd snuck into his empty church and lit a candle for his mother. He'd had faith then. Or at least he'd wanted to. He'd promised God that if his mom got well, he'd never doubt him again.

A cold sweat prickled around Miguel's hairline. Was God going to hold him to that?

"Here goes nothing," Leah whispered as she stepped off the elevator onto the fourth floor. Her peace offering nervously clutched in one hand, she paused a moment to get her bearings.

It was nearly ten o'clock Saturday night. The floor was silent except for the movement of the nurses behind the workstation to her right and the low drone of a wall-mounted TV to her left. Leah turned instinctively toward the television, hoping to find

Miguel in the waiting room. Instead she found Rosa with a magazine in her lap, staring into space.

"Hi, Rosa." Leah slipped into the chair beside hers and glanced around the lobby. No one was there but them. "How's your mom?"

"Still in surgery." Rosa reached up and pulled the pink scrunchie off her ponytail, shaking out her straight, shoulder-length black hair as if she had a headache. "Why did you come so late?"

Leah shrugged. "It's not that late, for a Saturday." It had been about four when she'd left Miguel's house, and she'd expected the surgery to be over by now. "When did she go in?"

"Around seven." Rosa rubbed her face and Leah could tell she was tired. "They had to do a bunch of stuff first, and the operation takes three to five hours. She could come out of surgery anytime now, or not until midnight. It's the waiting that's so hard, you know?"

Leah nodded, her heart going out to the younger girl. "Did you guys get any dinner? Where's Miguel?"

"Miguel!" Rosa rolled her brown eyes heavenward. "Check the cardiac ward. And no, we didn't get any dinner."

Leah handed her the Burger City bag she'd brought. "It's just burgers and fries, but I thought . . . I mean, I didn't know . . . Help yourself."

"Thanks!" Rosa took a Mega-Burger with cheese from the sack and began eating hungrily.

"So has, uh, has Miguel said anything about me?" Leah asked hesitantly.

"Like what?" Rosa asked, her attention on her french fries. When Leah didn't answer, though, Rosa looked into her eyes. "Like what?" she repeated curiously.

"Nothing in particular." As far as Leah could tell, Rosa didn't have a clue about her and Miguel's big blowup. "Do you know where he might be? Besides the cardiac ward, I mean."

Rosa smiled. "He's a nervous wreck. I tried to talk to him, but . . . you know Miguel. If his mind's made up to worry, then that's what he's going to do." She shook her head. "Maybe you can talk some sense into him."

Rosa took the package of fries she was eating out of the sack and handed the remaining food to Leah. "The last time I saw him, he was headed down that hall," she said, pointing. "I know he didn't go too far because he wouldn't risk missing the doctor."

Leah nodded and stood up. "Thanks," she said, wandering off with a white-knuckled grip on the bag. She had no idea how Miguel was going to react to her being there, but she had to try.

*He has every right to be mad at you for spying on him*, she reminded herself as she walked down the hall. *He has every right to break up with you, too, if that's what he wants to do.* But she had to be sure. She couldn't just let it go. Not like this.

She found him in the stairwell, gazing through a thin strip of window at the lights in the parking lot. He didn't turn around as she walked up behind him.

"Hi," she said softly. Nothing. It was as if she were talking to the window itself instead of the sullen guy it reflected. "I saw Rosa in the lobby."

He shrugged.

"She said your mom's still in surgery. I guess you're pretty scared."

"I'm not scared," he said, still not looking at her. "I'm worried, and that's not the same thing. What are you doing here, anyway?"

"Bringing you dinner?" Leah held up the bag of food hopefully.

"I already ate."

"That's funny. Rosa was starving."

"I'm not hungry, all right?" he said, turning around at last. His brown eyes were bloodshot. "I don't even know if I'm speaking to you."

Rebuffed, Leah set the bag on the floor. "All right. I'll go, then. I just thought you might need a friend."

He looked toward the stairwell door, as if to show her the exit. Leah felt tears rising again, clogging her throat. She couldn't say she didn't deserve the way he was treating her, but that only made things harder. She let her own gaze wander to the door and imagined it clicking shut behind her as she left, imagined never seeing him again . . .

The first tears spilled down her cheeks. She thought she'd cried herself dry earlier that evening, but now she realized that had only been the beginning. There would be days—no, weeks—of tears to come.

Impulsively she threw her arms around him, squeezing him tightly, breathing in his familiar scent one last time. "I'm so sorry," she said through her tears. "This is all my fault. I . . . I really hope everything turns out well for your mother—and for you. I'll be thinking about you every minute until I hear."

*And every minute afterward*, she almost added. But Miguel still hadn't moved. He held his strong body rigid, not giving in to her embrace. She closed her eyes and hugged him tighter. In her mind, it was the homecoming formal and they were on the dance floor again, oblivious to everyone else. She heard a slow song playing, felt the fabric of his black tuxedo beneath her fingers. More tears wet her cheeks. Then the music stopped. It was over. There was nothing to do but let go.

She dropped the embrace and took a faltering step backward. Before she'd retreated far enough to see his face, though, Miguel's arms shot out and caught her, pulling her back against him.

"Don't go," he said huskily. "I don't care anymore. I really don't. Just don't leave me here by myself."

She leaned against him, limp with relief. Her arms went around his shoulders, then his neck. Her cheek pressed his. Her lips found his mouth. She kissed him urgently, almost frantically, substituting kisses for the words that could never describe how she felt.

And Miguel kissed her back as if he understood.

"Are we okay, then?" she asked at last. Her voice trembled. "I mean, are we still together?"

He shrugged. "Do you want to be?"

"What do you think?"

"Well . . . I guess we're even," he said with a slight smile. "What is that now—one breakup apiece?"

He was referring to the time she'd broken up with him before Halloween. She couldn't believe he was joking about it.

"Very funny," she said, punching him in the shoulder.

"Oh, now you want to fight, do you?" He grabbed her fist and pinned it. Then, teasingly, he kissed her again.

She matched him kiss for kiss until her heart swelled within her and she felt light enough to float. Miguel finally knew her secret—that she had followed him around and spied on him—and they were still together. From here on out it would be nothing but the truth between them, no matter what. She never wanted to keep a secret from him again.

"So . . . should we go back and sit with Rosa?" Leah asked, stepping out of his grip.

Miguel turned instantly serious. "Yeah, let's. Someone ought to be telling us *something* soon. I can't believe how long this takes."

"I know." She slipped her hand into his. "I'm glad I came."

They stared at each other a moment, the enormity of the understatement hanging between them. Then they began to laugh.

"Yeah, me too," he chuckled, bending to retrieve the Burger City bag. He swung it up to sniff it as they pushed out the stairwell door into the hallway. "I'll be even gladder if you brought some ketchup for those fries."

"What a dump!"

Jesse Jones parked his BMW at the curb outside Charlie Johnson's house Sunday morning and checked the assignment sheet in his hand, praying he'd made a mistake. *435 West Rockford Street.* As near as he could tell, that was where he was. He had never been to this part of town before and none of it was nice, but the house he was parked in front of had to be the worst one on the block. Old and run-down, it featured a jungle of weeds and overgrown vegetation stretching from the rickety porch all the way down to the street.

*All it needs is a couple of old cars pulled to parts and strewn around everywhere*, Jesse thought disgustedly. *Maybe a truck up on blocks*. Then again, the senior citizen he'd been forced to help for his community service project was probably too old to dismantle cars.

Jesse reluctantly stepped out of his nice clean BMW and began making his way up the sidewalk to the house. The single-story building had been white once—sometime around the last ice age. Now the paint was partially peeling and partially hanging in shreds, exposing the rotting gray boards underneath. A whiff of mildew hung in the air, gaining strength as Jesse climbed the three wobbly stairs to the front porch. He wasn't sure if the smell was coming from under the house or if it was part of the house itself. Either way it wasn't pleasant, and Jesse imagined how much worse the odor would be in the hot, humid air of a Missouri summer.

*Before which I'll be long gone*, he promised himself. Coach Davis was making him do forty hours with this Charlie guy as a punishment for getting caught with alcohol at school, but it was only mid-November and Jesse had no intention of letting the coach's assignment linger on a single day longer than necessary.

He turned his back to the door and surveyed the yard again from the height of the porch. *This guy doesn't need his yard mowed*, he thought. *He needs it bulldozed!* The weeds alone were going to take a day to pull; all the bushes had to be cut back, there were dead tree branches lying around where they'd fallen, and, somewhere under that mess, Jesse supposed there was even grass.

*This bites*, he thought, wheeling back around and angrily punching the doorbell.

At first there was no answer. There was such a lengthy pause, in fact, that Jesse had half begun to hope the old guy wasn't home. Then he heard a noise—a curious, slow scraping—followed by a cheerful shout from inside. "I'm coming! Just give me a minute."

It seemed like much longer before the door finally opened. An extremely thin, extremely bent, white-haired old man leaned forward over an aluminum-frame walker, his ink-veined hands gripping the rails, his head bobbing slightly.

"Charlie Johnson?" Jesse asked, his spirits sinking even lower.

"You must be Jesse," the old man responded. "The agency told me you were coming." His blue eyes were piercing beneath his gray brows—the only part of his body that still had some spunk. "Come on in."

But Jesse couldn't come in, because Charlie's

17

walker was blocking the doorway. It took the guy somewhere between a minute and an hour to get turned around and shuffle toward the small living room. Jesse, already impatient, could barely restrain himself from pushing him along. Eventually Charlie made it to a worn brown recliner and, turning around yet again, lowered himself into it. He motioned for Jesse to take a seat on the lumpy sofa.

"So, what exactly are you going to be doing here?" Charlie asked.

"What?" Jesse was surprised by the question. "I don't know. I guess that's up to you."

Charlie shook his head. "How can I tell a volunteer what to do? You should do whatever you want."

*I want to leave,* Jesse thought, but he managed not to say it. "Well . . . your yard could use a little work."

A minute before, he'd been dreading tackling that mess, but compared to the cramped half-darkness of the living room, the yard seemed almost inviting. He wanted to get outside again, away from Charlie and the sickly whistle coming from his chest.

"They sent me a diplomat!" Charlie laughed. The laughter turned his whistle to a wheeze. "The yard looks like crap—you don't have to mince words with me, kid. I haven't been able to do anything out there for years, and as far as hiring a gardener goes . . ." He gestured around his shabby surroundings. "I'm not exactly rolling in money."

Jesse stood up abruptly, every breath Charlie took grating on his nerves. "Okay! Well, I brought some yard tools with me, so I guess I'll go get started." He moved eagerly toward the door.

"Forgive me if I don't get up, but—"

"No! Don't get up!" Jesse nearly shouted. "I mean, uh, I can let myself out."

"Leave the door unlocked so you can just walk back in if you need anything."

"Yeah, okay," Jesse agreed, although he couldn't imagine anything he'd need that Charlie might actually have. "I'll see you later."

"Come say good-bye before you go. You can lock the door then."

"Okay, okay," Jesse said, making his escape.

Back outside at last, he took a deep breath of cold fall air. The temperatures had been peaking in the low forties all week—freezing by California standards—but at that moment the chill seemed almost pleasant. Not that he was looking forward to his first winter in this godforsaken place. Jesse had only moved to Clearwater Crossing the previous spring, and he didn't even want to think about how its winter would compare to winters in Malibu, his hometown. It would snow at some point—he knew that—and he supposed there would be sleet. Rain had already been pounding the city off and on for weeks.

"I'd hate to be a mailman in this place," he grumbled as he headed down the porch stairs toward his car.

He unloaded a gasoline-powered weed whacker from the trunk and turned to face the yard again, wondering if he'd brought enough gas. He no longer thought it would take him all day to deal with the weeds out front. By the time he cut them, bagged them, and dragged them to the curb, he was pretty sure it would be more like two days.

*Fine. Whatever.* In a way it was better. He knew Coach Davis expected him to serve his community service sentence two or three hours at a time in short little visits after school, but Jesse saw no reason to drag things out. *This yard can keep me busy enough to knock out the whole forty hours in four or five long days.*

He pulled the starter cord on the weed whacker and immediately set to work. The sooner he put this depressing dump behind him, the better!

# Two

"Hi," Jenna said shyly, opening the passenger door of Peter's blue Toyota early Monday morning. She could feel herself blushing, which was ridiculous, but she couldn't help it. Ever since Peter had kissed her at the park on Saturday, he seemed almost like a stranger.

"Hi." Peter waited for her to buckle her seat belt, then pulled away from the curb and headed toward the high school. Jenna peeked at him as he drove. His eyes were on the road, his face relaxed, as if nothing were different between them.

But, of course, everything was different. They had talked for hours Saturday afternoon. To her amazement, Peter had said he'd had feelings for her for a while, that he'd only been waiting for a chance to tell her. She could barely believe it after she'd been so sure she was losing him to Melanie, but, at the same time, her heart had leapt. Because when Jenna started thinking about it, she realized she'd had feelings for Peter too. What else could explain her jealousy at having to share him?

Peter made the turn onto the main road. "Ready for school?" he asked.

"As ready as I ever am. You know I have that geometry test today. There ought to be a law against giving exams in first period—no one's even awake that early."

She had expected to get a chuckle, but Peter only nodded. *He's nervous too*, she realized.

Thank goodness they had agreed to take things slowly! Wondering if Peter was going to kiss her again—and when—would only have added to the weird new pressure on them both. Instead, they had agreed to go on acting like the friends they were, with the understanding that they were something much more now. And when they got used to that . . . well . . . she'd let him know.

"I guess lunch will be the best time to find everyone and remind them about the Eight Prime meeting at Melanie's house tomorrow," said Peter. "But if you see anyone before that, go ahead and grab them while you have the chance."

"I will," Jenna promised. Eight Prime was supposed to plan its pancake breakfast fund-raiser Tuesday night. It was the next step toward earning the bus for the Junior Explorers, the disadvantaged children's program Peter and his friend Chris Hobart ran; the bus was to be donated in the memory of Kurt Englbert, a classmate who had died in a car crash earlier that year. "Boy, this is a busy week!

Geometry today, Eight Prime tomorrow. And I have a choir rehearsal after school on Wednesday because our Thanksgiving concert is Saturday night."

"Next week won't be much quieter, between Thanksgiving and the pancake breakfast. Is Mary Beth coming home?"

Jenna made a face. "You know Mary Beth. My mom's been bugging her to commit, but she keeps saying she doesn't know if she can make it. She'll probably show up on our doorstep an hour before dinner and demand a drumstick, like she did last year."

Peter smiled. "It'll be good to see her again."

"If she comes," said Jenna. Her oldest sister was a junior at Tennessee State University. During her freshman year, she'd come home for every major holiday, and for summer too. Sophomore year she'd come home for Thanksgiving and Christmas, choosing to spend spring break with Nashville friends, and then she'd taken summer classes, which meant she'd only had two weeks off. And so far this year, Jenna couldn't remember even a phone call that her mother hadn't initiated.

Peter drove into the CCHS student parking lot and found an empty space. Other cars were pulling in all around them, and crowds of students hurried through the cold morning air toward the main building. Jenna climbed out of the Toyota and pulled her backpack up over one shoulder of her thick down jacket.

"Come on, Peter," she urged, suddenly in a hurry.

"I'm coming," he said as he locked the car doors. "What's the big rush?"

"I'm nervous about this test," she admitted.

They began crossing the asphalt toward the lawn in front of the high school. "You studied all day yesterday, right?"

"I know. But it's geometry."

The grass was silver with frost as they stepped onto the lawn. Jenna imagined it shattering under their weight.

*That's closer to me than Peter used to walk*, she realized as they headed toward the main building. Just a little closer. Just enough.

"You'll do fine," he said.

"I know." With a shy smile, Jenna let the back of her gloved hand brush against his.

Peter brushed back. Their knuckles kind of caught. It was crazy, but suddenly her heart was racing like anything. Side by side, hand to hand, they walked into the main hall.

"You kids ought to be in school," Mrs. del Rios protested again. Miguel and Rosa had just walked back into her room after an early lunch downstairs in the hospital cafeteria. "If you left now, you could still make it for afternoon classes."

She shook her head as she said it, though, and Miguel knew she didn't mind too much that they'd cut school that Monday. After all, this was a historic family event. Of course, she'd probably have been a little more concerned if she'd known he'd missed a geometry test that morning, but he'd figure out a way to make it up somehow. Everything would be fine.

He smiled. Everything was already fine.

The kidney transplant surgery had gone very well. Dr. Gibbons had been jubilant yesterday, and this morning even more so. The kidney was already functioning, and there were no early signs of rejection. Mrs. del Rios would have to take antirejection drugs for the rest of her life, but as long as her new kidney stayed healthy, she was done with dialysis. Despite some pain from the eight-inch incision the surgeon had made, she already claimed to be feeling better. And soon she'd be able to return to a practically normal lifestyle, with far fewer restrictions on her diet and activities.

"I can't wait until you come home, Mom," Rosa said, smiling.

Mrs. del Rios sighed happily. "Me either. But you heard the doctor. It won't be before next week. I wouldn't be much use to you at this point anyway—you saw me try to walk around the hall this morning."

"Don't you worry about anything," Miguel told her. "We've got everything under control. Besides, we're going to be here with you every day."

Mrs. del Rios raised her eyebrows. "You're going to be at *school* every day. Promise me you'll go tomorrow."

"But Mom . . . ," Rosa whined.

"I'll be here when you get out," Mrs. del Rios said. "You don't need to worry about me jogging off somewhere."

"All right, we'll go," Miguel said. "But only to make you happy."

"Thank you." Their mother relaxed back into the pillows. Miguel could tell she was tired, but under the pallor of the recent strain, her face shone with contentment. "This has been such a gift," she said dreamily. "Such an incredible gift. Soon I'll be able to work full-time again. Things can finally go back to normal."

Miguel was so taken up in imagining that really happening that, for a moment, he didn't realize his mother had drifted off to sleep. When he did, he motioned Rosa from the room and quietly closed the door behind them.

"Mom's doing great," Rosa whispered happily.

"Yeah." But as they dropped into their familiar seats in the waiting area, his mind was racing in a hundred different directions.

Until that moment, Miguel had been thinking of the surgery only in terms of his mother's future. He had wanted the kidney for *her*—so she could be well, so she could live a normal life. But now, in an instant, he realized his future had changed too. If his mom went back to work full-time, the family wouldn't need him to bring in nearly as much money as before to get back on its feet. He *could* go to college now—to community college, anyway.

*I don't necessarily have to be a contractor anymore*, he realized. Ever since Mr. del Rios had died of cancer three years earlier, Miguel had planned to follow in his father's footsteps—and make use of his father's industry connections. With the job experience Miguel already had, a career in construction had seemed like the fastest way to start bringing home head-of-household wages. And he wasn't opposed to working in construction. Unlike Leah's parents, who thought everyone had to go to college, Miguel was proud of his father and of what he'd so nearly accomplished.

But now . . . now his future was wide open. *I could be anything*, he thought with mounting excitement. *Anything I want.*

*What* do *I want?* It had been so long since he'd considered the question that he didn't have an answer. He didn't even have an idea, and the possibilities were so vast they were almost disorienting. But his grades were good. He'd kept up with his college-prep classes. . . .

Rosa switched on the television. A soap opera

blared from the set, and before she could turn it down Miguel had been startled back to Earth. He shook his head, as if awaking from a dream. Then he smiled.

*I'll think about it,* he promised himself.

He had the feeling he'd be thinking about it a lot.

"Great," Nicole Brewster grumbled. She glanced around the packed interior of the cafeteria, hoping to spot somebody to sit with. Ever since the weather had turned cold and forced everyone inside, it was doubly annoying when her best friend, Courtney Bell, ditched her to go off campus with her boyfriend, Jeff.

Nicole saw the cheerleaders at their usual table and a bunch of football players crammed in at the surrounding ones. She looked around for Peter and Jenna, but couldn't find them. At last she spotted a girl she sort of knew with an empty seat beside her. She hurried to take it before someone else could.

"Hi!" Nicole said brightly, dropping onto the bench with her sack lunch in her hands. "Is it okay if I sit here?"

The girl shrugged. "Fine with me. I was just leaving."

"Leaving? Lunch just started!"

The girl looked at her strangely. "I'm finished, all right? I've got things to do." A minute later she was gone.

Nicole opened her brown bag, trying her best to look as if she had things to do too. She had barely unwrapped her carrot sticks, though, when Jesse Jones plopped into the vacant seat beside her.

"Why are you hiding over here in the corner?" he asked, grinning. His brown hair was pushed back off his forehead, and his open letterman's jacket revealed only a red T-shirt, as if in defiance of the weather that had everyone else thinking flannel and down. He tossed his lunch onto the table, obviously planning to stay.

*We're only friends. He's just being friendly*, Nicole reminded herself quickly. But her heart still pounded like crazy. She knew it was going to be a while before she could look at Jesse and not feel her old crush kicking in.

"Courtney ditched me," she admitted. "How about you? Why aren't you eating with the team?"

"I just, uh, don't feel like it," he answered, casting a glance in that direction. His cool blue eyes gave away nothing, but Nicole knew him well enough by now to guess there was a problem. Jesse did everything for a reason.

She let her eyes follow his. Maybe he was looking at Melanie—the two of them still hadn't completely made up from the fight they'd had before Melanie's accident. On the other hand, he saw her all the time at Eight Prime events. Nicole didn't think he'd be avoiding Melanie.

29

And then she knew. She was positive, in fact. Jesse *was* avoiding someone—but it wasn't Melanie.

Nicole consciously widened her eyes, going for the most innocent look she could muster. "Talk to Vanessa lately?"

Jesse grimaced. "You had to ask."

She could barely keep from laughing. Two Saturdays before, Jesse had taken the cheerleading captain to the homecoming dance, partially to show off to the football team and partially to get out of having to take Nicole. But his scheme had backfired when Vanessa had gotten it into her head that Jesse had a more permanent relationship in mind—and started making plans accordingly. Nicole was ready to bet that Jesse still hadn't told Vanessa he wasn't about to ask her out again. "Just tell me this: Does she know yet?"

"I don't want to talk about Vanessa." He put his sandwich down and helped himself to one of her carrot sticks, biting into it with a loud crunch. "Anyway, she's the least of my problems this week."

Nicole cocked an interested eyebrow.

"Do you know where West Rockford Street is?"

"I think so. Why?"

"Coach Davis is making me do community service over there. He's got me doing yard work for some old coot named Charlie."

"Community service? What for?"

"You know, to get back on the team after my suspension. That's the rule." He paused, then looked at her intently. "Isn't it?"

Nicole shrugged. "Search me. I've done a lot of stupid things, but I've never gotten caught with liquor in my locker."

"Yeah. Thanks for reminding me."

Nicole smiled sweetly. Knowing that Jesse would never be her boyfriend made talking to him a lot more fun.

"Anyway, this Charlie guy is old. I mean, we're talking scary old. He's all bent over and he uses a walker—you know, one of those granny frames? I thought I was going to mow his lawn on Sunday. Instead, I ended up weed whacking everything in sight for eight solid hours, and when I was done I still expected Tarzan to come swinging through any second. I've got to go back next weekend and try to finish it."

"Again?" Nicole asked indignantly. "Did they know how long it was going to take when they sent you over to cut his grass?"

"They don't care, that's the thing. I've got to spend forty hours with the guy, and as long as I'm there doing something, I don't think anyone cares what it is. Not even Charlie."

"Then maybe you could do something easier," Nicole suggested. "Maybe the man's just lonely and would like to play cards or something."

Jesse made a face. "I'd rather work outside.

Charlie seems all right, but he's so pathetic with the walker and everything. And you can hear every breath he takes. I'm starting to wonder if getting back on the football team was even worth the trouble."

"What do you mean? Of course it was!"

"I don't know. There were only two games left in the season anyway, and we already lost the first one."

"That's crazy." Nicole took a sip of her diet soda. "You also only missed two games. Besides, the game this Friday is against Red River, which is only *the* biggest game of the year. And if we beat them, we'll be in the state finals. Isn't playing in the finals what you wanted all along?"

"Yeah. You're right," he admitted with a sigh.

Nicole was still basking in the glow of that acknowledgment when Peter and Jenna walked up behind them.

"Hi, you guys," Jenna said. Nicole detected a subtle wink.

*She thinks the two of us sitting together means something,* Nicole realized. Not that long ago, she'd confessed her crush on Jesse to Jenna. Now she'd have to find a chance to tell Jenna what had happened, and that she and Jesse were just friends.

"We're reminding everyone about the Eight Prime meeting at Melanie's poolhouse tomorrow," Peter told them. "Same drill as before."

"Okay. We'll be there." Nicole barely noticed she was answering for Jesse too.

Peter nodded. "Good. Well, we've got to find the others, so we'll see you guys later."

"Great," Jesse grumbled after they had gone. "Just what I need—*more* community service."

"Going to an Eight Prime meeting isn't exactly hard labor."

But in her heart, she half agreed with him. They still hadn't earned even fifty percent of that stupid bus—at this rate they'd be at it the rest of their lives. Nicole remembered the good old days, when she and Courtney had hit the mall nearly every weekend, and sighed with longing.

*At least I don't have two charities to deal with*, she thought, sneaking a sideways look at Jesse's profile.

Unexpectedly, her eyes crossed paths with a close-set pair scowling from several tables away. Vanessa Winters had spotted them. Nicole quickly averted her gaze, then turned her head so the other girl couldn't read her lips.

"Don't look now, but I think someone at the cheerleaders' table is jealous," she teased Jesse.

"Aw, geez. Is she looking this way?"

"Glaring this way, you mean. And yes, she is." Nicole knew it wasn't very nice of her, but it felt good to see someone else striking out with Jesse for a change. "Do you want me to put my arm around you and act all infatuated?" she asked, batting her eyes.

"Knock it off!" he said, glancing nervously back over his shoulder. "Man, Nicole, I think I liked you better when you were still kissing up to me."

The comment stung, but Nicole only tossed her blond hair and forced a big smile. "That's too bad, *friend*. Those days are over."

# *Three*

"I'm telling you, sausages are easier," Jesse insisted. "They take up less room on the griddle, for one thing, and you don't have to turn them—you just kind of roll 'em around."

"Bacon tastes better," Ben said, unmoved.

The two of them had been arguing for five minutes, ever since Peter had opened the subject of the pancake breakfast menu, and Melanie was losing patience.

"I like ham," she finally broke in, exasperated. "But it's not like this is everyone's last breakfast on Earth, so it doesn't really matter. Besides, Jesse's right—sausages will be easier."

Jesse looked amazed, then leaned back in his Hawaiian-print chair wearing a supremely self-satisfied expression. It was almost enough to make her change her mind in favor of bacon.

"Should we vote?" Peter suggested. "All those in favor of sausage?"

Everyone held up their hands, except for Ben,

35

who was being unusually stubborn, and Miguel, who hadn't come to the meeting.

"He wanted to stay at the hospital with his mother," Leah had explained when she'd arrived at the Andrewses' poolhouse, the last of the seven to get there. "She had a kidney transplant Saturday night."

"A kidney transplant!" Jenna had exclaimed.

"Thank God," Peter had murmured, briefly closing his eyes. Melanie had been as shocked as Jenna, as shocked as the rest of them, but something had told her Peter wasn't totally taken by surprise.

"Is she all right?" Melanie had asked. "I didn't know she was sick!"

Leah had rolled her eyes, but a happy smile had lit her pretty face. "That's Miguel's standard procedure—keep everyone on a need-to-know basis at all times. And yes, his mom is fine. She's doing really well, in fact."

"That's fantastic," Peter had said, rejoining the conversation. "Tell them our prayers are with them."

Leah had nodded. Melanie knew Leah wasn't religious either, but she never seemed bothered by comments like that. She always took them in stride.

"I will. He said to tell you he'll still help out with the breakfast. We're supposed to assign him a job."

"He should cook," Nicole had suggested. "He was good at that at Kurt's carnival."

"We'll probably all be cooking, at least part of the time," Peter had said. "So I guess we might as well start by figuring out what will be on the menu."

"Pancakes, scrambled eggs, and bacon," Ben had proposed immediately, as if he'd been waiting for the chance.

"Bacon makes a huge mess," Jesse had argued. "It splatters everywhere and you have to separate all those little tiny strips."

"Okay, it looks like sausage wins," Peter said now, counting the hands in the air. Leah held up two— one for her and one for Miguel. "Sorry, Ben."

"Bacon is better," he muttered, but he seemed resigned to the decision.

"Scrambled eggs are a good idea, though," Jenna said, obviously trying to cheer him up. She looked cute that night in a new blue sweater that matched her eyes, her thick brown hair falling halfway down her back. She held up the pen she always took notes with. "Or we could have fresh fruit."

"Instead of eggs?" Jesse exclaimed, scandalized. "Fruit's not food! It's more like decoration."

"You seem to have this all figured out, Jesse," Melanie said, playing with one of the marble-trimmed drink coasters. "What do you want to serve?"

"Pancakes, sausage, scrambled eggs, and orange juice. You can pretend the juice is liquid fruit," he added for Jenna's benefit.

"Actually, that sounds good to me," Leah said. "Fruit is nice, but it's so bulky and time-consuming to cut up, and we'd need so much of it. If we go with Jesse's menu, maybe we can put an orange slice on the plates, like they do in restaurants. That would look nice and tie in with the orange juice, too."

There was a lot more discussion before they finally agreed to adopt Jesse's suggestion, with the additions of milk for the kids and coffee for the adults. The date was set for two Saturdays away, on Thanksgiving weekend.

"I can make some posters and flyers," Jenna offered. "We should send flyers to all the churches in town, and maybe we can hang some posters at school. I guess we'd have to ask Principal Kelly, though."

"You do the flyers and I'll take care of the posters," Leah said, splitting the difference. The principal was a friend of her parents.

"Okay," Jenna agreed eagerly, writing down those assignments.

"We ought to try to get a notice in the newspaper again," Nicole piped up. "Why don't you call that woman who wrote about us last time, Peter?"

"I will. And I'll call that TV reporter who interviewed me about the city council budget scandal too. You never know—we might get some sort of mention."

"I'd rather have some sort of cash," Jesse griped. "I really thought the council would have to pay up after that story hit the airwaves."

"Me too," said Leah. "I think we all did."

"Haven't you heard *anything* from them about that, Peter?" Melanie asked.

He shook his head. "Not a word. But we weren't expecting any help from the city council when we started this project, so nothing has really changed."

"Except that your being on the news brought in a ton of extra money," Jenna reminded them all.

Melanie nodded. The first thing Peter had done when he'd arrived was pass out a treasury report that showed another $694 coming in at his church because of the television broadcast.

The meeting broke up a few minutes later. Everyone said good-bye and started filing out of the poolhouse, but Peter lagged behind.

"I'll be out in a second," he told Jenna, tossing her his keys. "Why don't you heat up the car?"

Jenna nodded. "Bye, Melanie," she called, waving.

"Bye."

Melanie waited until Jenna was out of earshot before she turned to Peter. "What's up?" she asked, her heart beating a little faster. Why did he want to see her privately? What did he want to say?

"Did I ever mention that Amy Robbins's father is a truck driver?" he asked.

"No," Melanie said, a little taken aback. Amy was Melanie's favorite kid in the Junior Explorers program, but all she knew about Amy's parents was that her mother had died of an overdose.

"Well, he is. And he's in kind of a mess right now. When he goes on long hauls, he has a woman who looks after Amy. But he's got a ten-day job coming up across Thanksgiving weekend, and his regular sitter is leaving to visit family out of town. She can't take Amy, and that leaves him without a sitter for the holiday."

"Uh-huh," said Melanie, not sure where all this was going.

"Well, the thing is, Amy wants you. Mr. Robbins has been trying to find an adult, but everyone's busy. And the more people who say no, the more Amy begs for you."

"That's so sweet!" Melanie cried, touched. "I'd love to take care of her!"

"Are you sure? Because her dad needs to know pretty quick. He called me this afternoon to ask if you were responsible and if I thought you'd want to do it."

"Of course I'm sure! But I'll have to ask my father, I guess. She'd be staying here, right?"

Peter nodded. "There has to be an adult around in case there's an accident or something. And Mr. Robbins would want to meet your dad, too."

That wasn't such good news. Then again, her father had been drinking less since she'd cracked her head open. And if he knew someone was coming . . .

"I don't see a problem with that. But I'll have to ask him," she repeated.

Peter took a scrap of paper out of the front pocket of his jeans and handed it to her. "Here's Mr. Robbins's phone number. I'll call him when I get home and tell him you're going to ask permission, and when you find out you can call and give him your answer, okay?"

"Yeah. Sure."

"I bet you and Amy will have a lot of fun together. She'd probably rather be with you than her regular sitter anyway."

Melanie smiled. "I hope my dad will let me do it. I'm practically positive he will."

"I hope so too." Peter started backing toward the door. "Well, Jenna's running the car and everything. . . . Maybe I'll see you at school tomorrow."

She wished he didn't have to go. She wished he didn't *want* to go. But Jenna was waiting . . . and she was holding him up.

"All right. See you."

Melanie stood staring at Peter's handwriting for a

long time after he had gone. Then, with a sigh, she put the slip of paper in her pocket and started cleaning up.

Jesse had planned to go straight home after football practice on Wednesday, but when he drove out of the CCHS parking lot, he found himself turning toward Charlie Johnson's house instead.

Before he'd left there on Sunday, he'd promised to take Charlie shopping the following weekend. "Better to do it today and get it over with," he muttered now as he cruised over to West Rockford Street. He'd be able to add a couple more hours to his total that way, and it wouldn't cut into his Saturday yard time. Besides, he was pretty sure Charlie wouldn't be busy. It was hard to imagine how he filled his days, living in that big house alone, barely able to get around.

*There's always TV*, Jesse supposed. But how many talk shows could one person watch?

Even though Charlie wasn't expecting him, he seemed delighted by Jesse's unscheduled appearance. "Come in! Come in!" he said, lifting one hand from his walker to beckon to Jesse. "How come you're all wet?"

"Huh? Oh." Jesse ran a hand through his recently shampooed hair. "Football practice. I just got out of the shower."

"Football, huh?" Charlie looked as though he were going to say more; then he turned his walker abruptly and started hobbling back to the living room. "So why are you here today?" he asked, his back still turned.

"You said you wanted to go to the grocery store, remember? I thought it would be better to do that now than this weekend." Jesse paused. "That is, uh, if you're free. Then I can spend all day Saturday in the yard again."

Charlie nodded, his blue eyes sharp in an otherwise bland face. "You did a good job out there."

Jesse smiled weakly, knowing *good* could only be relative. At least a person could get up the walkway without tripping now. "Want to get going?"

"Let me get my coupons."

Jesse shifted impatiently from foot to foot as Charlie rooted around in the kitchen. It figured the guy would use coupons—it wasn't embarrassing enough that they were bringing a walker. On the other hand, judging from the condition of the house, Charlie was probably pretty short on cash. The interior was better than the exterior—everything was reasonably neat, at least—but the brown furniture was worn, the walls were dingy, and the edges of the drapes were frayed and tattered. *It must be all he can do just to dust,* Jesse thought, wondering how the hardwood floors got swept.

"Okay, I'm ready," Charlie announced, coming back out of kitchen with a raggedy, paper-clipped stack of coupons.

"Does that, uh—does that thing fold up or something?" Jesse asked, gesturing to the walker.

"Yep. It'll fit right into your trunk, but I might need a hand down those stairs out front."

*Great.* Giving Charlie a hand would mean touching him, and Jesse really didn't want to do that. Not that Charlie was dirty—just old and frail, and about as worn around the edges as his living room furniture. Jesse briefly wondered where the guy's family was and why they weren't helping him out, but there wasn't even a photograph around to lend a clue. A second later, he put Charlie's potential relatives out of his mind. He wasn't going to be hanging around long enough to learn the guy's life story.

Out on the porch, Charlie managed to take the three stairs himself by holding tightly to the handrail. Jesse set the walker down at the bottom, and, after about a year, Charlie inched his way to the car. By the time the walker was in the trunk and Charlie was in the passenger seat, Jesse felt sure he could have already gone and come back on his own.

And that was nothing. At the grocery store, things got even more excruciating.

"You can't be too careful on this linoleum,"

Charlie insisted, moving his walker at a snail's pace while Jesse pushed a shopping cart. "People drop and spill stuff all the time. All I need is to step on some water or a grape and I'm in the hospital with a broken bone. Hey, how much is the mustard?"

Jesse grabbed the brand of Dijon that his family always ate. "Two eighty-nine."

"Are you crazy? You're just paying for the name! I want American mustard."

Jesse was pretty sure all mustard was French, but he didn't say so—he didn't have an extra hour for the discussion. Instead, he put the good mustard back and reached for a bright yellow jar.

"No! The store brand!" Charlie leaned over his walker to point to a generic-looking jar on the bottom shelf. "Brand names are all rip-offs."

Jesse picked up both the yellow jar and the generic one and compared the prices. "There's only fifteen cents' difference."

"Ha!" Charlie crowed triumphantly. "Told you!"

"But this is some brand no one's even heard of," Jesse protested. "At least with the other you know what you're getting."

"It's all the same. Mustard is mustard," Charlie declared. "Now, I need ketchup, too, and I have a coupon for ketchup." After about a century, his shaky old hands pulled a slip of paper from the stack. "Look for Del Monte, twenty-eight ounces."

Jesse put the cheapest mustard in the cart and found the Del Monte ketchup. "If you buy generic mustard, why not generic ketchup?" he asked, holding out the bottle for Charlie to inspect.

"Because with my coupon this brand and the store brand will cost the same."

"But if mustard is mustard, why isn't ketchup ketchup? Why not just buy the store brand of ketchup, too?"

Charlie looked at him as if he were dense. "Because I have a *coupon* for ketchup. Who does the shopping in your family?"

"My stepmother," Jesse lied. Elsa sent the housekeeper, but suddenly he didn't want Charlie to know that. It was too embarrassing to admit that his healthy young stepmother couldn't be bothered to buy groceries to an old guy dragging himself down the aisles in a walker.

Charlie shook his head. "Put that ketchup in the cart."

And condiments were only the first aisle. By the time they'd zigzagged through canned goods to bread, Jesse felt like picking Charlie up and strapping him into the shopping cart. It was torture shuffling down the seemingly innocent—ah, but deceptively deadly—linoleum with the guy, checking every price, finding every coupon. By the time they finally reached the cash register, Jesse was so frustrated he could barely keep from screaming. It was a relief to unload the groceries from the cart, and a double relief because he did it fast.

The checkout clerk was about nineteen and very good-looking. Jesse gave her the eye as he put Charlie's groceries on the conveyor belt and she smiled at him in return. Encouraged, he sauntered forward, planning his opening line.

"Jesse! Jesse, where did you put my ketchup coupon?" Charlie brayed suddenly behind him.

Jesse cringed. "I never touched it. You have it somewhere," he turned around to whisper, casting an embarrassed glance at the girl behind the register.

Charlie fumbled through his pile of coupons, which had somehow become mixed with his cash. "Oh, here it is." He extended the dog-eared old coupon to the cashier as if it were some rare and precious document. "Thirty cents off," he said proudly.

The girl took it and smiled at Jesse again. "Your grandfather is so cute," she told him, crinkling up her nose.

His grandfather? And if that weren't humiliating enough, she thought *Charlie* was the cute one.

In the fresh air of the parking lot, Jesse loaded the groceries and Charlie's walker into his trunk, his pride still smarting. Charlie kept a grip on the roof of the BMW and watched him suspiciously.

"Does your dad know you're driving his car?" he finally asked.

"For Pete's sake, Charlie, will you give me a break? I got this car for my sixteenth birthday."

Charlie made a face. "When was that? Last week?"

"Oh, you're hilarious," Jesse muttered, barely restraining himself from saying more.

At last they parked at Charlie's house. Charlie needed help up the porch stairs, but by then Jesse was so anxious to get out of there he would have carried him up on his shoulders if it would have hurried things along. He half pushed, half pulled Charlie into the house and set his walker inside the front door.

"I have to rest," Charlie said, out of breath, his chest nearly whistling "Dixie." He added, "Maybe you wouldn't mind putting those groceries away by yourself."

*Mind? I might get to leave before dark that way.*
"Sure, no problem," Jesse said eagerly.

Charlie took a few achingly slow steps forward and pointed through the open doorway into the kitchen. "It should be pretty straightforward—cold stuff in the refrigerator and everything else in the pantry. If you can't figure out where something goes, leave it on the counter and I'll get it later."

Jesse hurried back out to his car, bringing in as many bags as he could carry. It felt good to be moving at a normal pace again, and the fact that Charlie had intentionally purchased mostly heavy items didn't slow him down a bit. "I need to stock up on this stuff now," Charlie had explained as he picked out his canned goods, "while I have you to carry it for me."

By the time Jesse came in with the last set of bags, Charlie had made it to his favorite chair. He smiled wanly as Jesse walked through on his way to the kitchen.

Jesse put away the frozen food first, then the refrigerated items. He wasn't sure what Charlie did with his bread, so he left that on the counter. Turning to the double-wide pantry, he opened the doors and prepared to unload canned goods into the mostly empty space.

Mostly empty . . . except for the top shelf, which was loaded from wall to wall with such a diverse assortment of half-full liquor bottles that Jesse caught his breath. He'd never seen so much alcohol outside a liquor store. His father's stash paled in comparison.

Glancing quickly back over his shoulder, Jesse made sure Charlie couldn't see the open pantry from his chair. Then slowly, furtively, he rose up on his toes to get a better look. The bottles were old— coated in dust and wearing odd-looking labels. It seemed they hadn't been touched in years.

Jesse's heart pounded with excitement. *Charlie must be too old to drink anymore.*

And since he clearly wasn't using the stuff, there was no way he'd notice a little missing. Especially from one of those bottles in the back. As slowly as Charlie moved, it would be a piece of cake to sneak some when he wasn't looking.

*Hmm*, Jesse thought, beginning to put cans on the shelves. *There might be something in this job for me after all.*

# Four

Thursday evening Melanie fidgeted in her bedroom, bouncing back and forth between her bed, where she was supposedly working on an algebra assignment, and the plate-glass windows looking out over the front acres and private road into the Andrewses' large property. It was dark outside—dark enough that the windows showed her her own reflection more clearly than the world beyond.

She focused on her image, appraising it as if it belonged to someone else. *Good hair*, she allowed with a shrug of her slender shoulders. She felt the small spot on the back of her head that had been shaved after her cheerleading accident. It had already grown out an inch; soon it would blend with the rest of her blond mane. Her mouth was good too, she decided, soft and full-lipped like her mother's. But her light green eyes always seemed like a stranger's. When she looked into her eyes, she didn't see herself—what she saw was Melanie Andrews, CCHS's first-ever sophomore cheerleader. She flashed herself a big, fake smile. Yep. Melanie Andrews.

51

The doorbell rang downstairs, taking her by surprise. She had missed the car she'd been watching for.

"I'll get it!" she cried, running out of her room and down the curving marble staircase. She hit the entryway at the bottom so hard that her knees buckled beneath her and she nearly lost her balance.

"Take it easy," her dad advised, meeting her near the front door. He was dressed casually but nicely, in honor of the big occasion.

"I just want to make a good impression," she said nervously.

"You'll make a better one if you aren't all red in the face," he teased. He was sober. That was good.

Taking a deep breath, Melanie opened the front door. Amy Robbins and her father were standing on the doorstep.

"Hi, Amy!" Melanie cried, bending to greet the little girl.

Amy regarded her gravely, with round brown eyes. She looked up at the façade of the Andrewses' grandiose concrete-and-glass mansion, and back at Melanie as if she had never seen her before.

*She sees the stranger too*, Melanie couldn't help thinking. When she'd played with the Junior Explorers in the park or at Eight Prime events, she'd always been just plain Melanie. Here, surrounded by wealth, she could only be Melanie Andrews. Even Amy saw it.

"You must be Amy's father," Mr. Andrews said, stepping forward to shake the man's hand. "I'm Clay Andrews. Please come in."

"I'm Luke Robbins. Thank you."

They all filed into the formal living room, taking seats on the seldom-used white furniture. "So, Amy!" Melanie said cheerfully, trying to draw her friend out. "I can't wait to have you come stay with me."

Amy nodded silently, her eyes still as round as quarters. The house seemed to overwhelm her. For the first time Melanie wondered what Amy's house looked like.

"I would never have asked your daughter to baby-sit for so long or have imposed on you if I wasn't in such a bind," Mr. Robbins told Melanie's father. "Are you certain you don't mind? I hate to disrupt your holidays."

"Nah." Mr. Andrews waved the concern away. "Mel and I, we keep a pretty low profile during the holidays. Amy won't be disrupting a thing."

"It'll be *fun* to have her," Melanie put in. "We're going to do all kinds of things together." She smiled reassuringly at Amy, but Amy clung to her father's hand, still mum.

"I really do appreciate this." Mr. Robbins patted

his daughter's brown curls. "And Amy's a good little trouper to understand about Daddy's work."

He looked up again. "You never know, in my business. We don't always get the regular holidays."

Melanie nodded, imagining Mr. Robbins driving around the country in an eighteen-wheeler, hauling food, or merchandise, or maybe even livestock.

"So when will Amy be starting her stay?" Mr. Andrews asked. "Wednesday night?"

"Wednesday afternoon, if that's okay with you. Mrs. Covington, her usual sitter, will bring her over as soon as Melanie gets home from school, and she'll pick her up when she gets back from her trip Sunday night. That will be easiest, I hope. That way you won't have to worry about taking Amy to school—she'll just stay for the holiday while Mrs. Covington's out of town."

"That will be fine," Mr. Andrews said. "And please don't worry about a thing. Amy's in good hands here."

Mr. Robbins nodded gratefully, looking relieved. "Thank you, Clay."

Melanie tried another smile at Amy and this time got one in return. She couldn't wait until Wednesday, still nearly a week away, when her friend would come to visit.

She just hoped her father would keep his drinking to a minimum while Amy was around.

———

By the time Jesse found a place to park after the football game Friday night, it was so late he thought he'd be the last to arrive at the postgame party. Quickly he locked his car and headed across the parking lot toward the entrance of The Danger Zone, the combination pizza place and video arcade where CCHS students always gathered after the last game of the regular season. The crowd was larger when the Wildcats had won, he'd been told, and as he pushed through the revolving door he decided that must be correct. The crowd there to celebrate the Wildcats' win against Red River High School that night was enormous.

"Jesse! Jesse! Over here!" someone shouted.

He scanned the packed arcade and spotted Gary Baldwin and Barry Stein, part of a big group of football players waving him over. Jesse nodded across the sea of heads between them and started walking that way.

The noise all around him was deafening. The Danger Zone was a big barn of a room, with arcade games lining the walls and dining tables in the center. There were so many people there that most had no place to sit, and they crowded in everywhere—at, on, and between the tables, in any hint of a gap between games, wherever two feet could stand. Everyone was shouting to be heard above the music that blared from the overhead speakers, and the raised voices, bursts of laughter, and arcade sound effects all became a din that echoed and multiplied. Jesse threaded his way toward the Wildcats, disoriented by the noise. And even in that bedlam, he heard his name called from every side.

"Jones! Hey, Jones, way to go!"

"Jesse! Hi, Jesse!"

"Killer game, Jones!"

It took effort to keep his smile from turning smug as he wound his way through the crowd, nodding to those who called out. The Wildcats had pounded Red River—beaten the team to a pulp and strained it—and Jesse's three touchdowns and two interceptions had been the capstone of that effort. He was back—back as the biggest game's clear MVP—and the entire school had been there to see his triumph. How could he not walk taller as he drank in their admiration?

"Jesse!" a familiar voice called out close beside him. Leah had spotted him and was waving him over, along with Peter and Jenna.

Jesse glanced indecisively from his Eight Prime friends to his teammates, then made a sudden detour.

"Great game!" Peter said. "Way to end the season!"

"You were great," Jenna and Leah echoed. "Congratulations!"

Jesse nodded, although his cockiness had just lost some edge. Peter had seen him at his lowest—all of

Eight Prime had—but they had never shunned him, never acted as if he were less of a person because he'd fumbled a pass . . . or had been suspended from the team. There was something about that knowledge that brought Jesse back to Earth. He could boast to his teammates about his success, but not to Eight Prime. Not anymore.

"You guys! You guys!" Nicole cried, running up. "Courtney and Jeff just found us a table. Come sit with us, Jesse," she added. "We have a pitcher of Coke and there's a pizza coming."

"Thanks," he answered, tempted, "but the guys are all waiting for me." He tilted his head toward Barry and Gary, who were jumping up and down, trying to get his attention. "I ought to hang with the team tonight."

"Sure," said Peter. "Stop by later if you want." The four of them pushed off to meet Courtney and Jeff, and Jesse watched them go, half sorry he hadn't joined them.

On the other hand, this was his big night—and he could see Eight Prime anytime he wanted. Picking up the pace, he closed the distance to his teammates.

"Jesse!" Barry greeted him. "Who's the man?"

"You're the man!" Gary answered for him.

They were both smiling, slapping him on the back. Then the rest of the team descended. For a moment, it was green letterman's jackets as far as he could see. His still-damp hair was mussed by rough hands; his arms and shoulders were pummeled as his teammates shouted their gratitude. Everyone was talking to him now, all right. Their coolness of the last few weeks had melted like Sno-Kones in summer.

"We're going to kill 'em in the finals," Hank Lundgreen, their captain, predicted. "You keep playing that way, and we'll be state champions yet."

Jesse grinned. After all, it was only his due. No one had worked harder for the team than he had. No one had sweat more, accomplished more, come back from more.

At the same time, he wasn't enjoying the moment as much as he'd expected. He was a star again! Everyone loved him. People who'd barely looked his way for weeks were suddenly his best friends. It was what he'd wanted, what he'd worked for.

So why did it feel kind of hollow?

The music pumping through the loudspeakers suddenly switched off in midsong. The break in the noise made people stop talking and look around for the cause. It turned out to be the cheerleaders, all eight of whom were standing on a row of chairs in the middle of the room.

"Let's hear it for the Wildcats!" Vanessa yelled through her megaphone. The other girls started cheering, waving their arms overhead as much as they could without losing their balance. Soon the entire arcade was roaring: "Wildcats . . . Wildcats . . . *Wildcats!*"

"And who's our MVP?" Vanessa shouted.

"Jesse . . . Jesse . . . *Jesse!*" Half the school took up his name, chanting at the top of their lungs. It was embarrassing, but in the very best, life-should-always-be-so-embarrassing kind of way. Jesse felt his cheeks flush, but he jumped up on a chair and waved to the crowd anyway.

"See you at the state finals Friday!" Vanessa hollered for her finale.

The students yelled until the room shook, and then the music came back on. Jesse started to climb off his chair. At just that moment, his eyes locked with Vanessa's. She stared at him from across the room, her expression a mixture of hope and annoyance . . . and hope was winning out. Jesse froze, his heart speeding, before he looked quickly away. The next instant he swore at himself for his own stupidity.

*She saw you. She knows you saw her.* Avoiding Vanessa was becoming more difficult all the time. He didn't want anything to do with her, but he didn't want a scene, either. Especially not in public. *You should have smiled. A little. If you treat her like an acquaintance, maybe she'll get the idea.*

His feet were on the floor again and he looked back up, hoping to renew eye contact and belatedly carry out his idea. He got more than what he'd wanted.

Vanessa was on her way over, and the expression on her face was anything but amused. Her close-set eyes were narrow and her mouth was pinched—she looked ready for a showdown. For a second, he seriously considered trying to dodge her. Then he reconsidered. He couldn't avoid her forever. Besides, how big a scene would Vanessa want to make in front of all these people? As captain of the cheerleaders, she had a reputation to protect too.

He took a deep breath and flashed her a disarming smile. "Hey, Vee," he greeted her. "How's it going?"

She faltered. "All right."

"Better than all right, I hope. Come on! We're going to the finals!"

"Yeah," she said, smiling a little.

It was working—he was pretending that nothing was wrong, and she had no alternative but to buy it. A couple more minutes of small talk and he'd move on, free for the next two weeks. Eventually she'd get tired of the game. They always did. All but Nicole, anyway.

"So, I saw part of your halftime dance. You guys looked good. That new coach is paying off, huh?"

"Sandra?" Vanessa made a face. "She thinks she's God's gift to cheerleading."

*And so do you,* he thought, *which ought to make things pretty even.* Besides, he'd already figured out

Vanessa didn't like her new coach. He was just having a little fun.

Vanessa moved in closer, close enough to cup a hand to the side of his head. "I'm still waiting for you to call me," she said under cover of the surrounding racket.

Jesse squirmed at her directness. Most girls wouldn't come out and say something like that, no matter how long he left them hanging. "It's only been a couple of weeks."

"You said you were going to call soon. I don't know what *your* idea of soon is, but you're way past mine."

"Give me a break, Vee. I've been a little busy."

She gave him a hard look, then slipped her arm through his, moving in against him. "Well, we're together now."

Every muscle in Jesse's body went rigid. "We're not exactly together, Vanessa."

He felt her stiffen too. "What do you mean?"

He disentangled himself and put some distance between them. "Don't do that, all right? Everybody's watching."

"So what? You didn't mind at the dance."

"Maybe I just didn't want to say anything."

She drew back, eyes blazing. "Well, excuse me," she said angrily, "but most of the guys I date—"

"We aren't dating, Vanessa."

She stared. "What?"

"I mean we went out once—for the dance. Let's not turn it into a big deal."

"Are you kidding me?" Her voice had gone so low he couldn't hear it over the noise, but he read her lips loud and clear.

"I never said anything else," he reminded her.

"I get it. I was good enough when you needed a last-minute date to the dance, but now that you're MVP you're done with me?"

She was madder than he'd imagined possible. Jesse grimaced, but stuck to his guns.

"Actually, I was done with you way before I became MVP."

For a minute he thought she might slap him. Her eyes narrowed to slits and color flooded her pale cheeks. She stepped back, her hands clenching and unclenching. "You are going to be so sorry you said that," she spit at last. Then she spun on her heel and stormed off, pushing and shoving to clear a path.

*That's the end of that*, he thought. He hadn't intended to be so blunt, but she'd practically forced him to. And now that it was done, he wasn't sorry. Sorry he hadn't been a little kinder maybe, but not sorry it was over. Besides, maybe it was better he hadn't let her down easily. He'd tried that after the dance, and look what had happened. There wouldn't be any confusion this time.

"What'd you say to Vanessa?" Barry Stein bent

closer to yell. "Whatever it was, I don't think she liked it."

"Nothing," Jesse lied, glad they hadn't been overheard. Barry had been standing as close as anyone—if he hadn't managed to eavesdrop, then probably no one had.

"She seemed pretty steamed."

"She'll get over it."

Jesse knew Barry was right. Whatever Vanessa had felt for him, it certainly wasn't love. In fact, he was pretty sure she'd been using him the same way he'd used her. So then why the final threat? He shook his head. *She was just trying to save face*.

And then he saw Melanie, looking right at him, hands on her hips. When their eyes met, she tossed her head and turned her back.

*Great*, he thought. He had a feeling she'd seen the whole thing, and he wondered what she thought had happened.

The first tiny stab of fear pierced his heart. He wondered what Vanessa would *tell* her had happened.

By the time the CCHS Thanksgiving concert finally started, Jenna was already tired. She'd spent that Saturday morning helping Peter with the Junior Explorers, and when she'd come home there was barely time to do her homework, wash her hair, and eat dinner before the Conrad family was piling

63

into her dad's big van for the drive to school. Now she stood backstage with the rest of the jittery choir, listening to the school's concert band wind up its last piece. And, in spite of everything she'd done that day, she felt her energy surge back in one excited rush at the thought of singing in front of all those people.

"Are you nervous?" Ginny Peters whispered.

"A little," Jenna admitted. "I sing in church every Sunday, so I shouldn't be, but this is a much bigger group, and they haven't all heard me a hundred times."

Ginny shuddered, rubbing her hands up and down her arms. "I'd be dying if I had to sing a solo—I'm nervous enough already! But you have nothing to worry about, Jenna. You and Ron sounded awesome at the rehearsal."

"Thank you!" Jenna said, touched by the unexpected compliment.

"Look sharp!" their choir director, Mr. Evans, hissed suddenly. The band had stopped playing. "Everyone, look sharp."

He waved frantically for the choir to begin filing onto the stage from one side while the band exited at the other. Jenna took her place and gazed out over the sea of people in the school auditorium, a nervous smile firmly in place. The building was full of parents and friends, but she couldn't make out individual faces because of the lights focused on the stage, dazzling the performers and leaving the audience in semidarkness. She knew her family and Peter were out there somewhere, though, and she cranked up her smile a notch in case they were watching.

Mr. Evans came out in front of the group and raised his hands, and the next thing Jenna knew, she was singing. They all were, performing the songs that by now were routine. All their hard work and practice was paying off in a nearly flawless performance, and Jenna felt her heart lift higher with every note. By the time her duet with Ron Holder came up—"Someday" from *West Side Story*—she felt as if she couldn't miss. She sang her part with feeling, with confidence, and Ron answered with depth and strength. Then there was one more number with the whole choir, the big finale, and that was it. Soon Jenna found herself filing offstage with the rest of the choir, thunderous applause filling her ears.

"Congratulations!" Ginny said when they were back in the wings. "You were great!"

Jenna smiled her thanks, not trusting her voice. It was strange, but now that the performance was over, she felt far more nervous than before it had begun. Her knees were suddenly shaky, her palms damp, and her stomach was doing flip-flops. She had always been that way—cool in an emergency and emotional afterward—but she was still taken by surprise by the way her body was betraying her. Especially when things had gone so well.

And then she caught sight of Peter's familiar face peeking around the stage door. His dark blond hair spilled onto his forehead and his blue eyes sparkled with mischief. "Peter!" she cried, running to him. "How did you get back here?"

"I know people," he said mysteriously. "Come on, we're all going for ice cream. Your family is meeting us there."

In Peter's car, on the way to the ice cream parlor, Jenna started feeling like herself again.

"I was really nervous," she confessed. "Not so much before, but afterward I felt almost dizzy."

"You sounded great. Everyone in the audience loved your duet with Ron. They were all talking about you guys when the lights came up."

"They were?"

He smiled. "It made me proud. I mean, I was always proud of your singing. But especially now, because, well . . . you know."

"Yeah." Her heart was suddenly pounding even harder than when she'd left the stage.

At the ice cream parlor, her family had already found a table large enough for the eight of them. She and Peter slid into seats near the end and everybody ordered. Jenna wondered if her family could see anything different about her and Peter—if they had guessed at the change in their relationship. If they had, no one said anything. At first the conversation was all about the concert. Then, halfway through the sundaes, it turned to the upcoming holiday.

"I'm so glad Mary Beth decided to come home for Thanksgiving after all," Mrs. Conrad said, a glow in her tired eyes. "I can't wait to see her."

Jenna glanced toward Caitlin, expecting her to be happier still. When Mary Beth had lived at home, Caitlin had clung to her older sister like shrink-wrap.

"I'm going to take her to work and show her around," Caitlin said proudly. "Dr. Campbell said I could."

Jenna smiled and ate her last bite of ice cream. Eighteen-year-old Caitlin was blooming at her new job as a veterinarian's assistant. Every night at dinner she was so full of stories about her day that it was hard to believe she was the same shy girl who'd once barely spoken at all.

"How come you're taking her and not us?" Maggie demanded. "Allison and I want to see."

"Me too," said Sarah. There was a smudge of hot fudge on her bottom lip.

"You do?" Caitlin seemed surprised. "Well, okay.

But I can't take everyone all at once. It might be disruptive to the animals."

*To say the least*, Jenna thought. Maggie was thirteen, Allison twelve, and Sarah ten. Not only that, but Maggie and Allison got pretty silly whenever they were together.

"You girls can see Dr. Campbell's office anytime," Mr. Conrad pointed out from the other end of the table. "Mary Beth is only going to be here four days."

"I promise I'll take you soon, though," Caitlin told them. "We're going to be closed on Thursday, but I'm still going to have to go in to check on the animals that are boarding. Maybe I can take one of you with me then."

"Speaking of animals, what are you planning to do about that stray?" Mrs. Conrad asked, referring to the dog Caitlin had brought home on Halloween. "Why don't you leave it at the vet's next weekend? I don't want that animal scrounging around the house while I'm trying to serve a turkey."

"Mom!" Caitlin protested. "Abby always stays in the garage. She's not going to be any trouble."

Mrs. Conrad glanced at her husband, then sighed and turned back to Caitlin. "It's been almost a month, Caitlin. I've tried to be patient, but you have to find that dog a permanent home. That was the agreement when I let it stay, and you knew it. The animal's well now. There's no more reason to wait."

Caitlin put down her spoon. "I have found a home for Abby—mine."

"What? Caitlin—"

"Let me finish, Mom," Caitlin interrupted. "I love Abby. I don't want to give her up. And by January I'll be able to afford my own place. You *have* been patient, but if you could just give me a little more time, I'll move out and take Abby with me."

No one said anything for a minute. Jenna looked from her sister to her parents to Peter. He shrugged, as much at a loss as any of them.

"Caitlin! You're moving out?" Jenna whined.

Caitlin nodded. "Aren't you happy for me?"

Jenna had expected to be thrilled when this day finally came. Not only would she have her own bedroom, she wouldn't have to feel guilty about taking it away from Caitlin anymore. But instead all she felt was regret. Over the last two months, she'd grown much closer to her older sister. *I'm going to miss her*, she realized. *I'm going to miss her a lot.*

"I guess so," she answered uncertainly.

"January's a long way away," Mr. Conrad said firmly. "We can talk about this later."

"But what about Abby?" Caitlin insisted.

Mrs. Conrad seemed a little shaken. She smoothed her auburn hair with one distracted hand. "She can stay in the garage until then, I suppose."

Caitlin smiled. "Thanks, Mom. Thanks, Dad."

When they left, Peter drove Jenna home even though she could have ridden with her family. She knew he wanted to see her alone for a few minutes, but she wasn't very good company. She was so distracted by thoughts of Caitlin that she barely noticed when they pulled up at the curb in front of her house.

"I'll walk you to the door," Peter offered, snapping her out of her stupor.

"What? Oh. You don't have to," she said automatically, unbuckling her seat belt.

"Jenna . . . I know I don't *have* to."

"Oh. Right."

Her pulse was too fast again by the time they reached her front door. "Well, I guess I'll see you at church tomorrow," she said awkwardly. She hated that she felt shy around him, but it was hard getting used to the way things had changed.

"Okay." Peter looked at her expectantly.

*What?* she thought. He couldn't be expecting to kiss her, because they'd already talked about that. *Maybe he's expecting me to kiss him!* she thought. *Or shake his hand or . . . I don't know.*

"Good night, then," she said.

"Good night."

She turned her back to open the door, then impulsively spun around to hug him. It was a quick hug—more of a squeeze, really—but Peter seemed satisfied. He smiled broadly as she let him go and rushed into the house. She closed the front door, then sagged against it weakly.

*If I was really in love with Peter, would I be this freaked out about hugging him?* she wondered. On the other hand, she'd never had a boyfriend before, never been kissed—not really. And she and Peter had been friends for so long. . . .

*It's natural to be nervous*, she decided. *I'll get over it.*

She smiled to herself as she pushed off from the door and climbed the stairs to her third-floor bedroom. *Besides, just because I was nervous doesn't mean I didn't like it.*

# Five

When Leah walked into Mrs. del Rios's hospital room late Sunday morning, she found quite a crowd. Miguel's mother was propped up in bed, talking cheerfully to two women seated in chairs. A priest in a white collar and black shirt stood behind them, listening. Miguel was standing on the side of the bed near the doorway, his back turned toward her.

"Hi," she whispered, sneaking up and slipping her arms around him. "Did I come at a bad time?"

He squirmed out of her grip and turned around. "Leah!" he whispered, embarrassed. He glanced significantly back over his shoulder. "There's a priest here."

"I see that," she said with a grin. "In fact, he's kind of hard to miss."

He made a face to let her know she was mortifying him.

"Leah! How are you?" His mother had noticed her.

"Fine, Mrs. del Rios." Leah left Miguel to step forward to the bedside. "How are you? You look better."

Mrs. del Rios put a self-conscious hand to her loose, pillow-mussed hair. "Well, it's nice of you to say so. I *feel* better, anyway." She turned back to her guests. "This is my son's girlfriend, Leah."

"Nice to meet you," Leah murmured, nodding.

"And Father Sebastian from our church," Mrs. del Rios added.

"Hello, Father."

"Pleased to meet you, Leah," Father Sebastian returned warmly. "We were all just talking about when Mariana would be going home."

"Wednesday," Miguel put in quickly, stepping up to Leah's side. "Dr. Gibbons promised it would be Wednesday at the latest, so Mom could be home for the holiday."

"Oh, Mariana!" one of the ladies said. "I'm so happy for you. We all miss you at church, but we're so grateful you got your transplant."

"It's an answered prayer," the other agreed.

Mrs. del Rios smiled. "I'll be back at mass soon," she promised. "Next Sunday, if all goes well."

"Don't rush," Father Sebastian said. "We want to see you, but we want to see you healthy."

"But you must need me in the office!" Mrs. del Rios protested. "I've been out so long already." She worked at her church part-time, answering telephones and doing other clerical duties.

Miguel tensed, as if about to argue, but Father Sebastian took up the cause. "Not at all, Mariana.

Of course we miss you, but I have offers of help for as long as you're out. Please don't worry about us."

Miguel relaxed. "Come on," he whispered to Leah. "Let's go walk around."

They excused themselves and escaped into the hall, but instead of heading for the privacy of the familiar stairwell, Miguel led her in the opposite direction.

"Where's Rosa?" Leah asked.

"She stayed home this morning and went to mass. Then she was going to meet some friends. It's been tough for her, spending so much time here. And now that we're sure Mom's all right . . ."

They held hands as they walked, going nowhere in particular. It occurred to Leah that Miguel had probably gotten into the habit of wandering the halls as a way of stretching his legs.

"I bet you'll be glad to see this place in your rearview mirror," she ventured, gesturing with one hand to the hospital around them.

"Yeah. I'll definitely be glad to have my mom home again. But the hospital's not so bad—not if you're not a patient, I mean. There's always something interesting going on here."

He turned to face her, his dark eyes intent. "Life-and-death interesting, you know? Everything here seems so much more important than what happens everywhere else."

"Well, I guess a lot of it is. But it probably gets

pretty old if you have to be around it all the time. And not every visit turns out as well as your mother's. You have to hand it to the people who work here day after day. They must see it all."

Miguel nodded. "I think I'd like to work here."

"You would?"

He seemed as surprised as she was. "Yeah. I didn't know I was going to say that . . . but yeah. I think so."

Leah didn't know how to respond. Miguel had told her he wanted to be a contractor, like his father. He'd said he wanted to go to work right out of high school so he could get his family off public assistance. Leah supposed he could get some type of job at the hospital without a college education— something clerical or janitorial. But Miguel had spoken of life and death, and that didn't sound like mopping floors to Leah. That sounded like a doctor or a nurse, someone with a degree.

"There's no reason you couldn't work in a hospital if that's what you want to do," she said slowly.

He shrugged, then smiled. "We'll see," he said mysteriously.

Jenna's mother poked her head through the doorway of the back room where Jenna was hanging up her choir robe. "Are you riding home with Peter?" she asked. "Or do you want us to wait for you?"

"No. Go ahead," Jenna said quickly. "I don't know how long this is going to take."

Reverend Thompson had announced Eight Prime's upcoming pancake breakfast at the end of that morning's services, and now Peter and Jenna were supposed to meet with a few members of the Breakfast Boosters, the group of volunteers who usually organized the church's breakfast fund-raisers. Jenna finished hanging her robe and ran eagerly to Fellowship Hall, where Peter was waiting for her by the door.

"Did I miss anything?" she whispered.

"No. We were waiting for you to get here."

At a table near the center of the spacious room, three members of the Breakfast Boosters were sipping coffee from paper cups and chatting about the increasingly cold weather. Jenna recognized Mr. and Mrs. Howard and Maya Allen, a thirty-something single woman famous for her potluck desserts.

"Hi, everyone," Jenna said, approaching them. "Sorry about the holdup."

"No problem," Mrs. Howard said kindly. She and her husband were both white haired, but still full of energy. "Are you ready now?"

"Ready and reporting for duty!" Jenna replied with a playful salute.

The trio at the table stood up.

"You'll want to set up all the tables and chairs on Friday," Maya started off. She gestured around the large hall, which currently contained only a few scattered rectangular tables and the small stage at one end. "You've been to pancake breakfasts here before, I'm sure."

"Lots of them," Peter said.

"Then you know how we usually set up the tables. You get the most seating as well as the best traffic flow if you put them end to end in rows the long way. Set up your trash cans near the exit door and people can bus their own tables on their way out."

"We usually use the plates themselves for tickets," Mr. Howard said. "When people pay for their breakfast, they get a paper plate. At the front of the line, they hand it over and you fill it up. It's easier—it saves the extra step of collecting tickets later."

"Good idea," said Jenna, wishing she'd brought her steno pad so she could take notes.

"You're serving buffet style, right?" Mrs. Howard asked.

Jenna had no idea. She looked at Peter.

"All right," he said, with a grin that made it clear he hadn't thought about it either.

"Buffet is best," Mrs. Howard assured him. "Once everyone buys their plates at the entrance, they all just file up here and get served." She led them to a long pass-through between the hall and the adjacent kitchen. "They pick their drinks up there." She pointed, then walked to a second, smaller pass-through. "And after that they can go sit anywhere they want."

"What are you serving for drinks?" Maya asked.

"Orange juice, milk, and coffee," Jenna said, happy to finally know an answer.

Mr. Howard nodded. "You need to assign one person to coffee full-time. All they'll do is walk around with a pot and refill cups."

Jenna and Peter looked at each other in mock horror. "Not Ben," they said in unison. Ben was the clumsiest member of Eight Prime by far.

"One of us Boosters can do that for you, if you want," Maya offered. "We're all going to be here anyway, to make sure things go smoothly."

"But you're not going to be working!" Jenna protested.

"We were planning on it," Mrs. Howard said. "At least a few of us. You'll need a full-time person to sell tickets, one to pour all the drinks and set them out, one to refill coffee, one to wipe up tables as people leave, one to handle spills and other disasters, and at least one to serve each type of food. With only eight people in your group, that leaves you a little short of cooks."

"I see your point," Peter said quickly. "We'll definitely appreciate whatever help you can give us."

Mr. Howard smiled and nodded. "Then why not let me and some of the men take care of setting up the furniture Friday night? We've done it so many times before, it won't take us more than an hour."

"And on the day of the breakfast, why don't you kids focus on cooking and serving?" his wife suggested. "We Boosters can sell the plates, pour the coffee, and keep things running in the hall."

"Thank you," Jenna said gratefully. Eight Prime could all work in the kitchen that way. It would be more fun to be together.

"And don't forget that even with the men setting up your furniture, you'll still have to arrange with Reverend Thompson to get in here sometime Friday," Maya reminded them. "You'll have to buy your groceries that day and put them all away."

"Groceries!" Peter exclaimed, a slight groan in his voice. "We still have to figure out how much to buy."

Maya laughed. "It's not that bad. We have a standard shopping list, if you want to use it. It tells how much of each thing to buy for each one hundred people. You have to guess how many are going to show up, but after that, it's just a little multiplication."

"Yes!" Jenna said immediately. "I mean, yes, we want that, please."

"You'll do fine," Mrs. Howard told her, with a reassuring pat on the shoulder. "Come on, let's take a look at the kitchen."

---

"*You were there when I needed you,*" Miguel sang along with the radio as he drove home from the hospital. He felt good—better than he had in longer than he could remember. His mom was doing great, his future was wide open, and the blue November sky was so clear that the edge of every remaining leaf looked crisp and sharp as a razor. He was only a block from home, thinking about his conversation with Leah that morning, when the last sight he'd ever expected met his disbelieving eyes. Jesse Jones was attempting to mow the thigh-high lawn in front of Charlie Johnson's old place.

On impulse, Miguel steered to the curb, getting out of the car almost before he knew he was going to stop. The smell of gasoline and cut grass assaulted his nostrils. A rake lay across the sidewalk beside three full bags of leaves. "Jesse!" he called out, waving to attract his friend's attention over the roar of the mower. "Hey, Jesse!"

Jesse turned his head and saw Miguel. The motor sputtered to a stop. "What are you doing here?" he asked, confused.

"You first," Miguel countered, laughing. "I'm dying to know how Charlie roped you into this."

"You know Charlie?"

Miguel shrugged. "I know him to say hello to. He's lived here forever, and I just live right over there." He turned and pointed to the housing authority project across the street.

"Where?" Jesse asked. "Which house?"

"The one with the streetlight in front. Not that it matters—they're all pretty much the same."

But if Jesse knew Miguel was pointing to public housing, he didn't let on. And Miguel suddenly realized he didn't care one way or the other. They were as good as out of there now anyway—the whole world could know, for all he cared.

"So how about you and Charlie? Did he hire you or something?" Miguel asked dubiously. "With my schedule, I've never been able to lend a hand."

"Ha!" Jesse snorted. "There's not that much money in the world! No, this was Coach Davis's genius idea: forty hours of community service in exchange for letting me back on the team. That's the rule, you know."

"It is?"

"Isn't it?"

"I don't know."

Jesse's eyes narrowed suspiciously and his straight brown brows drew together. "If I find out Coach made this up . . ."

He shook off the thought and gestured around Charlie's huge front yard. "Do you have any idea how much work this has been?" he demanded. "I've been busting my butt out here for two days now, and the place still looks like a tornado hit."

"It doesn't look good," Miguel said.

Jesse shot him an evil look.

"What? You said it first!"

"Well, you weren't supposed to agree with me."

"Sorry." Miguel held out upturned hands. "Anyway, the yard does look better. It's the house that looks bad now."

Jess turned and surveyed his work. "Maybe I shouldn't have cut those bushes back so far," he conceded. "At least they helped hide how badly the place needs paint."

"Half those boards under the porch are rotten. I can tell from here. I'll bet you I could put my foot through that whole right-hand side."

"Don't demonstrate!" Jesse said quickly. "Geez, that's *all* I need."

# Six

"I can't believe we're actually here together," Nicole teased as she and Courtney walked down the mall's main promenade after school on Monday. "You're absolutely, positively *sure* Jeff isn't free?"

Courtney scowled impatiently and tossed her bright red hair. "I can call him and check, if you want. You can take the bus home."

"Yeah, very funny. You have to admit you've been practically glued to the guy lately, Court. I barely even see you."

"That's not because of Jeff. If you weren't with the God Squad from dawn till dusk, maybe we'd have more time."

Now it was Nicole's turn to look impatient. Courtney had pinned that name on Peter and Jenna just because they went to church and didn't try to hide it. "Aren't you bored with calling them that? I mean, at first it was mildly amusing, but now it's getting old."

Courtney rolled her eyes. "Maybe because now it's getting personal."

"What's that supposed to mean?"

"You know what it means—you're one of them, Nicole! Pretty soon you'll be trying to drag me off to church again or something."

Courtney had been an atheist for as long as Nicole had known her. And it was true that in the early days she had made a few attempts to bring her friend to Sunday school, but she had long since given up. It was too weird, now that she was older, trying to talk to people about God. Especially when she knew they didn't want to hear it.

"If that's what you're worried about, why aren't you worried about Jeff doing the same thing?" Nicole retorted. "He's been friends with Peter and Jenna longer than I have."

She had expected an argument, but Courtney only sighed. "I know. Sometimes I think he ought to go out with you instead of me."

"*What*? I thought you guys were doing great!"

"We are. I guess. Oh, look at that cute dress!" Courtney changed direction and walked closer to the store window, pulling Nicole along behind her. "How are things with Jesse?" she asked, changing the subject.

"If you have to ask, that proves you haven't been spending enough time with me lately. I told you Jesse and I are just friends now."

"Yeah, you say a lot of things," Courtney replied, a little of her feistiness returning.

"I mean it," Nicole insisted. "I've got better things to do with my time."

Courtney didn't stifle her laugh. "Like what?"

"Like . . . stuff," Nicole replied, deciding against mentioning fund-raising with Eight Prime.

Courtney smiled slyly. "So you're really through with Jesse? No final secret hopes?"

There was always *hope*. "None," Nicole lied.

"Good. Then you can do me a favor."

Courtney put on a big, this-is-your-lucky-day kind of smile that made the hair on the back of Nicole's neck stand up.

"What kind of favor?" she asked suspiciously.

"Jeff has this friend he's been bugging me to fix up with someone so we can double-date. And now that you're back in the game . . ."

"A blind date? No way!"

"Oh, come on. You'll like him."

"Why don't I believe you?"

Courtney pulled her over to a bench and sat her down. "Okay, I lied. The guy's so religious, he makes the God Squad seem low-key. But who else am I going to fix him up with?"

"Way to sell him, Court." Nicole rolled her eyes. "I'm totally interested."

"Come on, Nicole," Courtney begged. "Just go

out with him once. One time. You're the only person I know who even has a chance of getting through an evening without telling him how full of it he is."

"No, Courtney! If he's so horrible, why do you want me to go out with him?"

"Because, for some inexplicable reason, Jeff likes the guy. And I like Jeff, all right? Come on, Nicole, be a friend." She was whining now, tugging on Nicole's sweater sleeve. "*Please.*"

It wasn't like Courtney to be so needy. To hear her say please was even more unusual. It felt good to have her friend's full attention again, even if the favor she'd asked for was awful.

"All right," Nicole said, relenting. "But I'm warning you, Court, he'd better not be weird. And it's a double date, right? I'm not going out with him alone. And I'm not going anywhere romantic. A movie or something—that's it."

Courtney smiled triumphantly. "Any more conditions?"

"Yeah. You're paying."

By the time cheerleading practice had ended on Monday, there was no doubt left in Melanie's mind—Jesse had dumped Vanessa. In contrast to her ridiculously over-the-top, I'm-so-happy behavior of the week before, the squad captain had been a witch to everyone all afternoon. Except to Melanie.

She wouldn't even look at Melanie. The moment Sandra had dismissed them, Melanie had grabbed her things and run, unable to get out of there fast enough.

*I knew this was going to happen*, she thought, hiking her gym bag higher on her shoulder as she hurried to the bus stop. *I knew it, I knew it, I knew it.*

Not that she really cared. Vanessa had been getting gradually ruder all year. Being ignored by her would be an improvement. And it wasn't as if Vanessa could kick her off the squad anymore—they had Sandra to run things now. *Lucky for Jesse*, Melanie thought. *He could have really messed things up for me.*

She still didn't understand why he'd gone out with Vanessa in the first place. Anyone could have seen it was a terrible idea. Apparently he wasn't too good at picking out potential girlfriends. Nicole had been too immature for him. Vanessa hadn't been smart enough. And Melanie . . . Melanie hadn't been interested. Of course, those were just the girls she knew about.

*I'll bet his girlfriends are like roaches*, Melanie speculated, smiling at the thought. *For every one you see, there's a hundred more you don't.*

She was almost to the bus stop when a red BMW sped by and stopped at the intersection. *Speak of the devil . . .*

"Jesse! Hey, Jesse!" she called, running to catch up.

There were cars behind him at the stop sign, but he ignored them. Melanie reached the passenger door and yanked it open.

"Miss your bus?" he asked sarcastically.

"You owe me," she informed him, tossing her gym bag into the backseat and climbing in. She slammed the car door. "Okay, drive."

"Not that I need to be blackmailed to do a friend a favor, but—just out of curiosity—exactly *why* do I owe you?" he asked, turning toward her house.

He was bluffing. Melanie could see by his eyes that he already knew. "Why don't you tell me?"

"I didn't think you were even speaking to me."

"Now, Jesse, you know that's not true," she said sweetly. "I spoke to both you *and* Vanessa at the homecoming dance."

"Oh."

"That's all you're going to say?" she demanded. "What were you thinking, Jesse? You knew she was going to take it out on me!"

"No, I didn't," he said, becoming testy himself. "I just asked her out on one date. How was I supposed to know she'd go totally delusional on me?"

"Because she's *Vanessa*. Didn't you figure that out the first time? After your little one-on-one at the lake?" It was a low blow but Melanie couldn't resist.

"Don't make me sick. Look, if it'll make you happy, I'll never go out with another girl in Clear-

88

water Crossing, all right? I'll be a monk until I graduate and get out of this backward town."

Melanie laughed sarcastically. "Like I really believe that."

"Believe it," Jesse said darkly. "I'd already half decided that anyway. Everything is such a big deal to you people. Every little thing, I swear. You'd all have heart attacks if you moved to California."

"Boy, somebody's in a bad mood." She had intended to give him a seriously hard time about Vanessa—not so much because she cared as because he deserved it—but with Jesse already so low, taking him down had lost most of its thrill.

"You'd be in a bad mood too if you were me. I'm not exactly having a year to remember here in the Show Me State." He grimaced, and for the first time Melanie noticed how tired he looked. "Which is to say, I'll definitely remember it—just not the way I wanted to."

"It can't be that bad."

Jesse simply glanced at her, his disgusted expression saying it all.

"Come on. You guys killed Red River last week."

"Yeah. That was all right."

Melanie couldn't believe it. He wasn't going to brag about being MVP? Wasn't going to point out he'd practically won the game single-handedly? She snuck a sideways look at him. His straight brows were drawn low over sullen blue eyes; his jaw was a tight, hard line. No, apparently he wasn't.

At the beginning of the year, he'd have bent her ear about it all the way home. *And he would have stopped the car to pick me up instead of making me chase him.* After which he'd have tried to pick her up for real. Of course, she and Jesse had been fighting all year, so it wasn't surprising he'd given up on her.

*No. It is.* Not because she thought she was so great, but because she couldn't have imagined Jesse giving up on anything. Mr. Confidence was always strutting around with his ego just barely in check. She glanced at him again. He seemed different now. Tired. The worse for wear. There was barely a trace of his old cockiness.

And she missed it, she realized. Not the bragging, necessarily, but the self-assurance that had gone with it. In a way, she even missed having him follow her around, making his futile passes.

"What are you thinking?" Jesse asked.

"Nothing," she answered quickly. "Nothing at all."

"Can I talk to you?" Jenna asked her mother late Tuesday afternoon. Her father and Caitlin were still at work, and Maggie, Allison, and Sarah were playing upstairs, making far too much noise to hear anything else. If she hurried, she might actually be able to squeeze in a private conversation.

90

Mrs. Conrad looked up from the meat loaf she was making and wiped her hands on a kitchen towel. "Sure. What's up?"

Jenna glanced back toward the doorway. The coast was still clear. "I have an idea," she announced in hushed tones.

"Ooh, sounds scary," her mother teased. "How about giving me a hand with the green beans?"

The vegetables were draining in the sink. Jenna shook the excess water from the colander and began snapping them into a cooking pot. "I don't want Caitlin to move out," she said abruptly.

"Excuse me?" Mrs. Conrad said. "I'd have sworn you were the one who couldn't wait to get her out of here."

Jenna felt her cheeks turning red, but she couldn't say she didn't deserve it. She *had* been in a hurry for Caitlin to leave. Once.

"That was before, Mom. You know I'm sorry about the way I acted. I've done everything I can to make it up to her."

"I know," her mother admitted. "And I think it's made a difference, too. The two of you have become good friends."

"That's right! And that's why I want her to stay. You know she'll be happier with us than out all by herself."

Mrs. Conrad plunged her hands back into her half-mixed meat loaf. "I want her to stay too. But

Caitlin's an adult now. She has to be allowed to grow up and make her own decisions."

"Sure, but we have to help her to make the right one!"

"And you think you know what that is." There was a trace of a smile on her mother's lips.

Jenna abandoned the beans. "Just hear me out," she pleaded. "I have a plan that's guaranteed to keep Caitlin at home."

# Seven

"Careful! Careful, Mom!" Miguel said worriedly. "Here, don't try to get out by yourself."

He leaned in over the passenger seat of his old car and tried to get a decent grip on his mother, one that would allow him to hoist her onto the sidewalk without making her scream in pain.

"I'm okay, Miguel," she laughed, stepping out to the curb on her own. "Dr. Gibbons wouldn't have let me come home if I wasn't."

"Dr. Gibbons!" Miguel harrumphed, unwilling to admit that his opinion of the too-young, redheaded doctor had changed immensely for the good.

Inside, Rosa was waiting for them. "Welcome home, Mom!" she cried. She rushed forward to hug their mother gently, then gestured around the living room with pride. "Miguel and I are going to take care of you. Look."

Miguel let his eyes roam the room as he guided his mom to the sofa. Rosa had done a first-class job of straightening up and decorating. A big WELCOME HOME banner hung on the wall opposite the couch, a small vase of fresh flowers graced the coffee table, and a TV tray had been stocked with all their mother's special needs: the prescriptions Miguel had filled, a box of Kleenex, a pitcher of water with a glass, and a stack of dog-eared paperbacks from the lending library at their church. A thick blanket and pillow rested at one end of the sofa, a pair of soft new slippers at the other. He and Rosa had gone halves on the slippers from their meager savings accounts.

"Oh! Oh, you two. You didn't need to do all this." Mrs. del Rios was clearly moved. Tears pooled in her brown eyes, threatening to spill over.

"We wanted to," Rosa said simply. "We're so grateful to have you home. Tomorrow will be the best Thanksgiving ever."

She picked up the blanket and settled it over her mother's knees, then dropped onto the couch beside her. "I can't believe you're finally well," she said, throwing her arms around her mother and burying her head on her shoulder. Her voice broke on the last word, though, and for a moment none of them could speak.

At last, Mrs. del Rios pulled a tissue from the box on the TV tray and wiped her wet eyes. She handed one to Rosa as well. "Do you want one, Miguel?"

"No need," he said gruffly, turning his head to wipe his eyes on his sleeve. When he faced his mother again, she was smiling.

"This *will* be a special Thanksgiving," she said. "I know I'll never forget it. I only wish I was a little more mobile so I could do the shopping and cook a turkey dinner. I don't know what we'll eat."

"Please, Mom!" said Miguel. "We have a lot more to be thankful for this year than a stupid turkey. We can eat popcorn, for all I care."

"The pilgrims did," Rosa pointed out with a mischievous smile. "The Native Americans invented it."

Miguel rolled his eyes. "Thanks for the history lesson. You know what I meant."

"I could make a macaroni-and-cheese casserole," Rosa offered. She was just learning how to cook, and that was her best dish.

"Sounds fine to me," Miguel said. "I'll make a salad to go with it."

Mrs. del Rios smiled. "Under the circumstances, I think macaroni and cheese will be positively delicious."

"I don't understand," Jesse said, trying to keep his temper in check. "If you didn't want to buy a turkey or something for Thanksgiving, why did we have to come to the store *today*?"

He looked around impatiently at the droves of harried shoppers that had flooded the supermarket that afternoon. People were loading their carts to the brim, frantically stocking up for the big feast the next day, and between the shoppers and the holiday displays, a healthy young person could barely fight his way down the aisles. A person with a linoleum-defying grip on a bulky aluminum walker had no chance at all.

"Crowds don't bother me," Charlie returned calmly. "I'm in no hurry."

"That's good." Jesse could no longer control his sarcasm. "Because we're going to be here all night."

Charlie picked up a miniature can of peas and checked the price. He hesitated, then put it back on the shelf. They moved an inch forward, to the canned lima beans. Then the corn.

"Why don't you just get a turkey like everybody else?" Jesse finally exploded. "You're killing me, Charlie, I swear."

Charlie put down the corn and fixed him with sharp eyes. "If you didn't want to come here, why did you suggest it?"

"I *thought* you might need some groceries. After all, it is Thanksgiving tomorrow." Jesse glanced down at the small plastic grocery basket dangling from his hand: a navel orange, a carton of yogurt, and a can of soup. "This isn't exactly what I had in mind."

He could hardly tell Charlie that what he'd really had in mind was helping himself to some of his liquor when he unpacked the bags. With all the unwelcome family togetherness Jesse anticipated over the next few days, he had a feeling he was going to need it, and while he'd guessed that an old guy on his own probably didn't go through food too fast, this was ridiculous. It had been a week since the last time they'd come, and Jesse could eat what was in the basket so far for a snack.

"It might have occurred to you that a turkey and all the trimmings would be a little much for me to manage, let alone eat by myself," Charlie said.

It might have—if Jesse had been thinking of anything beyond replenishing his vodka supply. He shrugged sullenly and followed in silence as Charlie scrutinized the rest of the vegetables and finally selected a can of succotash.

*Ooh, two for one,* Jesse thought sarcastically, putting the corn-and-lima-bean mixture in his basket.

Finally they made it to the end of the store. Charlie shuffled down the last aisle and picked out a package of cookies. At the end of the aisle, though, instead of turning back, toward the cash registers, he kept going, directing his walker into the corner liquor section.

Jesse perked up immediately. What was he up to now? Getting a bottle of champagne, maybe, for the holiday? But Charlie bypassed the wines and champagnes, going straight to the hard liquor. He stopped his walker in front of the densely packed wall and stood staring at the bottles. Jesse's curiosity had reached the boiling point by the time Charlie finally spoke.

"Did you know I was an alcoholic?" Charlie asked casually. "Was. Am. It's all the same, I guess."

"You?" Jesse gasped, taken totally by surprise. "But you're so old!"

"Probably not as old as you think," Charlie said, a wry smile on his face. "Drinking takes a toll, you know. It does things to your body if you keep at it year after year. Between that and . . . well . . . it takes a toll."

Jesse nodded, speechless.

"I was a horrible liar when I was drinking," Charlie added, gazing longingly at the bottles. "Always trying to cover my own guilty tracks. I couldn't keep a job, let alone a wife. In the end it almost killed me." He sighed. "I haven't taken a drink for fifteen years, but I still keep all the liquor I had in the house the day I quit, as a reminder of how it nearly cost me everything."

Jesse heard Charlie's words with a growing sense of discomfort. *Why is he telling me this?* he wondered. His eyes scanned nervously around them to see if anyone else was listening.

"A lot of people, they give up the drink and they want it gone," Charlie continued conversationally. "They go on one last binge, or they pour it down the sink. Out of sight, out of mind, they think. But

I knew it would never be out of my mind for five minutes. So I kept it. Kind of a trophy, I guess. Kind of a monument to what a man can do if he has to."

He turned to Jesse, his blue eyes so intense they glittered. "Know what I mean?"

"Uh, yeah. Well, I—I mean, I guess so," Jesse stammered. Thoughts were running through his head so fast, he could barely think at all.

*There's no way I can sneak any liquor from that pantry—Charlie's been memorizing those bottles for fifteen years. And why did he bring up such a personal subject anyway? He must know.* But what did Charlie know? *He knows I'm not mowing his lawn out of the kindness of my heart, that's for sure.*

Charlie's eyes still bored into his.

*Did Coach Davis tell him I was suspended for drinking? Did he set me up with Charlie on purpose?* Jesse was already half convinced the coach had lied about the community service rule; from there it was a short leap to imagine the coach fixing him up with an alcoholic.

He shifted his weight and looked away, toward the registers. "Come on. Let's pay and get out of here."

Charlie didn't say much in the car on the way home. The trip seemed to have exhausted him. Jesse stole occasional glances his way, just to make sure he was still breathing.

*It would be kind of sad to be that old and all alone,*

he thought. He wondered what had made Charlie quit drinking. Was it just bad health, or had there been some major, defining moment when he'd realized he couldn't do it anymore? And that part about not keeping a job . . . where had Charlie worked? He'd said he couldn't keep a wife, either. Had he been married? Did he have kids? If he did, they must not live in town, or else why would he have to rely on Jesse for such basic things as yard work and transportation?

Guilt pricked Jesse's conscience. It wasn't as if he'd been so nice about helping out, either. He snuck another look at Charlie. The old man was dozing off, his white hair stark against the black leather seat.

*He ought to have a turkey*, Jesse thought. Who knew how many more Thanksgivings the guy would live to see?

"So! What should we do first?" Melanie asked Amy, crouching beside her in an attempt to make the Andrewses' cavernous entryway less scary. Wednesday had finally arrived, and Mrs. Covington had just dropped the little girl off.

Amy stared back mutely, her brown eyes round. At last her small shoulders shrugged. She seemed almost more overwhelmed than she'd been the night she'd come with her father.

"Is it the house?" Melanie asked. "It's the house, right?"

"Your house is big," Amy whispered.

"I know. It is. But you'll get used to it, and then it will be fun. We can play hide-and-seek. Would you like that?"

Amy nodded uncertainly, and Melanie took her by the hand. "Come on. Let's go put your suitcase in my room."

As they climbed the curving marble staircase, Melanie tried to see the house through Amy's eyes. On their right, the raw gray concrete rose two stories high, the expanse of wall interrupted only by the numerous framed paintings by Melanie's mother. Underfoot, the marble stairs were broad and polished to a glassy shine. And off to the left, the stairway fell away to the entryway, also gleaming marble, and the formal, white-carpeted living room beyond, farther and farther below as they climbed. The landing at the top of the stairs was dominated by huge plate-glass windows with a view of the swimming pool and the back acres of the Andrewses' large property. The pair saw only a glimpse of the large rectangular pool, poolhouse, and fields and trees beyond, however, before they turned left down the hall, then left again, and arrived at Melanie's room.

"Here we are!" Melanie said cheerfully, hearing

the strain in her own voice. Dealing with Amy in this new environment was awkward, especially with Amy acting so shy. "Look, I set up a cot for you next to my bed." She could have put Amy in a real bed in one of several spare rooms, but she didn't want her guest to be scared, all alone in the big house.

Amy took a few steps forward into Melanie's suite. Melanie watched as her eyes raked over the cot and queen-sized bed, Melanie's childhood doll collection, and the big picture windows, then dropped to the snowy white carpet.

"Let's put your suitcase under your cot, all right?" Melanie removed the rectangular, cloth-covered case from Amy's unresisting hand and slipped it underneath in one smooth motion. "If you want, we can unpack that later." She took a few steps across the large room and opened the white louvered doors of her walk-in closet. "We ought to be able to find some room in here somewhere," she joked, gesturing around the enormous space.

Amy followed her over and stepped inside. "These are all your clothes?" she asked, awestruck.

"Yep. See something you want to try on?"

For the first time since she'd arrived, a familiar sparkle lit Amy's eyes. "You mean it?"

"Sure. We can play dress-up, if you want." For a moment, Melanie considered dragging her mother's evening gowns into it, then changed her mind—

she wouldn't risk damaging those. But she had something of her own a first-grader might like even better. Reaching toward a rack, she pulled out a couple of hangers. "Want to try on my cheerleading outfit?" she asked, holding up the sweater in one hand and the short pleated skirt in the other.

Amy's eyes became huge. Without a word she shrugged her coat off onto the floor and pulled her pink sweater over her head, stripping to her undershirt. Melanie helped her put on the CCHS sweater, then the skirt. The skirt hit the girl below the knees and Melanie had to bunch the too-loose waistband together with a hair clip. The sweater sleeves hung well past Amy's hands, but she seemed quite pleased with her reflection in Melanie's full-length mirror.

Melanie rolled up the sleeves and handed Amy a set of pom-poms. "Now, say, 'Go, Wildcats!' " she instructed, raising a fist for Amy to copy.

"Go, Wildcats," Amy complied.

"Go, Wildcats!" Melanie repeated, more loudly.

"Go, Wildcats!" Amy hollered.

"Go, Wildcats!" Melanie shouted, throwing in a little jump.

"Go, Wildcats! Go, Wildcats! Go, Wildcats!" Amy screamed, leaping around like crazy, a big grin on her face.

"Come on. Leave the pom-poms here and I'll show you where the bathrooms are," Melanie said, relieved to see her young friend back to normal. "We've got bathrooms all over the house."

She started with the one adjoining her bedroom, then took Amy around the rest of the upstairs, leaving out her father's bedroom and her mother's art studio. The doors to those rooms were always closed. Downstairs, they saw everything except her father's study, because Mr. Andrews was in there, and the den, because Melanie was sure he'd end up there later. They ended their tour in the kitchen. Melanie opened the door of the oversized stainless-steel refrigerator and let Amy look inside.

"See anything you like?"

The temperature in the fridge must have risen fifteen degrees before Amy finally selected a juice box from the stock Mrs. Murphy had brought in for the special weekend. Melanie grabbed a Diet Coke and shepherded her minicheerleader to the leather furniture in the sitting area off the kitchen.

"Wow! Is that your pool? Can we go swimming?" Amy asked in a rush, running to the sitting room windows. She pressed up against the glass, getting her first good look.

Melanie laughed. "Swimming? Are you nuts? It's freezing out there."

Amy thought that over. "We could swim with our clothes on."

"No way, José. Maybe you can come back and

104

swim this summer, but no one's going in that pool this week."

Amy's expression implied she'd never heard more tragic news. The effect was hard to take seriously, though, in combination with the oversized cheerleader outfit.

"I'll tell you what we *can* do. How'd you like to order a pizza?"

"Now?" Amy glanced back through the glass at the still-light afternoon. "It's too early for dinner."

"Not if we're hungry, it isn't. We can eat whenever we want to."

Amy left the windows and plopped down on the pale leather sofa at Melanie's side. "I like extra cheese," she confided.

Melanie reached for the cordless phone on the coffee table.

"Wait. Don't you have to ask your dad first?"

"Ask him what?"

Amy glanced nervously down the hall in the direction of Mr. Andrews's study. "Ask him if it's okay," she whispered.

Melanie smiled. "Nope. I'm allowed to order pizza whenever I want to."

"Cool!" said Amy, visibly impressed.

Melanie placed an order for a pizza with extra cheese, then set up a game of checkers on the table to amuse them while they waited for the delivery person.

"Do you have to ask your dad if you want to stay up late?" Amy wondered, moving a black checker.

"No."

"If you want to watch TV?"

Melanie laughed and moved red. "Of course not! I'm too old for stuff like that. My dad lets me do what I want."

"Wow," Amy said with a sigh. "I have to ask my daddy practically everything. I don't mind, though," she added quickly. "He mostly usually says yes. He just wants to take care of me, you know, now that Mommy is gone."

"That's right. He wants to make sure you're safe, because he loves you."

"My daddy loves me a lot," Amy said confidently, moving another checker. "More than anything. He'll never, ever leave me, either. Not like Mommy. Your move, Melanie. Why aren't you moving?"

"Huh? Oh." Melanie moved a checker without thinking. Her mind was stuck on what Amy had told her. Their situations were so much alike, and yet . . .

*I wish I could say the same thing,* she thought sadly. She knew her father loved her, but more than anything? Enough to never leave her?

She wished.

He didn't even love her enough to quit drinking.

106

# Eight

Nicole heard the phone ring, but she didn't get up. Her mom was already banging around in the kitchen, fooling with the pots and pans, and Nicole was watching the Macy's Thanksgiving Day Parade with Heather.

She got up fast enough, though, when she found out who was calling.

"Nicole!" Mrs. Brewster hollered impatiently. "It's Jesse!"

"Coming!" Nicole screamed, leaping to her feet. There was a phone in the basement rec room, but no way was she going to talk in front of her nosy little sister. Instead she ran up the stairs to the kitchen and took the call there.

"Hi, Jesse. What's up?" she asked, doing her best to sound cool. *Only friends, only friends* ran through her head as she spoke, like canned music in an elevator.

"Do you know how to cook a turkey?" Jesse asked.

"A turkey?" Nicole laughed nervously, her eyes on the pale, goose-bump-covered monster her mother was wrestling stuffing into at the other end of the room. "You mean like the *whole* turkey?"

"No, just the feet," Jesse replied impatiently. "Of course the whole turkey—what do you think?"

Nicole had no idea how to cook a turkey. She had only recently mastered frozen turkey potpies. "Well, I never actually—"

"It doesn't matter. Just get over here, can you?"

"I don't even know where you are."

"I'm at Charlie's house. I told you that!"

He hadn't, but Nicole didn't argue—he already sounded about two steps from the edge. He gave her Charlie's address and begged her to hurry.

It took a certain amount of doing to get her mother to let her go out on Thanksgiving Day, but the Brewsters' dinner was hours away and Mrs. Brewster finally relented. She even agreed to let Nicole use her car. "Heaven knows I'm not going anywhere," she sighed, her manicured hand still buried inside the turkey.

Nicole raced upstairs to get dressed. She always watched the parade in her pajamas, but now she needed an outfit that would make the right impression—fast! She finally decided on black cords and a red sweater, and, even though she and Jesse were just friends, she brushed and spritzed her hair and secured the front with two red barrettes. Almost before she knew it, she was pulling up outside Charlie's run-down wooden house.

*No wonder they sent Jesse over here to do yard work*, she thought, looking around as she made her way up the cracked walkway to the front porch. *I don't think forty hours is going to be enough.*

The stairs to the porch were rickety, the railing loose. Nicole knocked tentatively at the front door.

Jesse yanked it open. "Finally!" he exclaimed, grabbing her by one arm and pulling her inside. "Nicole, this is Charlie. Charlie, Nicole."

Nicole barely caught a glimpse of a white-haired old man in a recliner before Jesse was hustling her into the kitchen. "Nice to meet you," she called over her shoulder, waving. But when she turned around and got her first good look at the kitchen, she could hardly believe her eyes.

"What are you *doing* in here?" she exclaimed.

"I don't know, all right? That's the whole point."

Nicole slowly surveyed the room, her eyes growing wider by the second. The L-shaped counter was littered with food, grocery bags, package wrappers, and what looked like pumpkin pie filling. A puddle of creamy orange liquid held a prominent place near the center of the counter, and splashes of the goo were everywhere. The edge of the pond dripped down to feed a smaller pool on the floor, like some sort of gross waterfall. A butcher-block worktable in the center of the room was similarly covered with food and debris, the focal point there being a huge raw turkey.

"It looks like a bomb went off in here."

"Yeah. Funny," Jesse said over the football game blaring from a portable TV wedged in next to the sink. "Don't just stand there and give me your critique—do something."

Nicole walked over and turned down the volume. "Like what?"

"Like . . . like . . . something!" he sputtered, at a loss. "I just wanted to surprise Charlie by making him a turkey dinner."

"He'll be surprised if he comes in here." Nicole picked up a sponge and swiped delicately at the puddle on the counter. "What is this stuff?"

"It's not radioactive, if that's what you're worried about," he said, nodding at the way she was holding the sponge by two fingers. "It's just pumpkin pie mix. I opened the can and then I picked up the turkey and—"

"*Voilà!*" Nicole finished.

Jesse winced. "Something like that. I would have cleaned it up, but I have to get this turkey in the oven *now* if it's going to be done today. Do you have any idea how long it takes to cook a turkey?" he demanded.

"Uh, a long time." She didn't want to admit that she still didn't know.

"A heck of a long time!" Jesse corrected. "Even longer, if you stuff it." He held up a dripping wad of plastic, the mangled wrapper the turkey had come in. "And these directions *stink*. They barely tell you anything."

Nicole shrugged helplessly. "Maybe you shouldn't stuff it, then. My grandmother used to cook the stuffing in a dish on the side."

"Really? Okay, good idea. What are you doing?" he added suddenly, looking up from his prostrate turkey.

She was wiping up the pie spill—more confidently, now that she knew what it was.

"Listen, forget about the pie, Nicole. How about helping me out with the yams?" He extended a big reddish lump of a vegetable in her direction.

"What's that?" she asked, throwing the sponge into the sink.

"Hel-*lo*!" Jesse said, staring at her as if she were dense. "It's a yam."

"That is *not* a yam, Jesse," she said with conviction. "Yams come in a can."

They faced off across the mess of a kitchen, Nicole with her hands on her slender hips. Slowly Jesse lowered the hand with the alleged yam in it to the table, defeated. "I have no idea what I'm doing," he admitted. "And I'm just going out on a limb here, but my guess is neither do you."

"I tried to tell—"

"Never mind," he interrupted. "Just help me think. What are we going to do?"

Nicole chewed her bottom lip. "We could call someone who knows how to cook."

"Yes! Good!" he exclaimed, pointing at her with that indecent red tuber. "Who should we call?"

"Jenna?" Nicole suggested. She had no idea whether Jenna knew how to cook or not, but she seemed like the type, if anyone did.

"No, she's too far away. We'll call Miguel."

Jesse wiped his hands on a soiled kitchen towel, then took Miguel's phone number out of his wallet. Nicole returned to the pie mess while he dialed the phone. She got the counter wiped up and most of the goop off the floor and cabinets before Jesse hung up.

"He's coming over," Jesse announced.

"Then the least we can do is get this place cleaned up before he gets here. And I want to watch the parade," she added, reaching to change the channel on the television.

"Don't you—"

The look she threw him stopped him short. "If I can wipe up pie goop for you . . ."

"Oh, all right," he muttered irritably.

By the time Miguel knocked at the door a few

minutes later, Nicole had found a plastic bag and picked up all the loose wrappers and trash, and Jesse had used up half a roll of paper towels washing away the residual stickiness from his pumpkin pie disaster. Nicole had also taken stock of the groceries Jesse had brought over that morning, arranging them neatly on the counter. She'd found a bag of potatoes, two of Jesse's so-called yams, a box of stuffing mix, a jar of gravy, a bunch of carrots, a bag of green beans, a can of cranberry sauce, a tube of refrigerated biscuit dough, and a ready-made pie crust with nothing to put in it.

"I can't stay," Miguel was already protesting as Jesse propelled him into the kitchen. "It's Thanksgiving and my mom just got home from the hospital."

"How is she?" asked Nicole.

"Good," he said, smiling broadly.

Nicole couldn't help noticing how handsome he was, with his dark hair and clear brown eyes. He was tall, too, and more muscular than most high-school guys.

*Leah was smart to snag him*, Nicole thought, half wishing she'd tried it herself. Then she glanced at Jesse and sighed. She'd been a little busy at the time.

"Okay! So how about this turkey?" Jesse steered Miguel toward the table.

Miguel held out the two items he'd brought with

him—a turkey baster and a meat thermometer. "My mom said to make sure all the plastic innards bags are out of the cavities, put the thermometer in, and just squirt the juices over the top once in a while until it gets to the right temperature. That's all there is to it."

"Wait a minute. Cavities?" Jesse asked.

Miguel flipped the turkey over, sank his fingers into a hidden hole under the neck, and extracted a lumpy plastic bag.

"Rookie mistake," he said with another smile. "My mother warned me. She said she cooked her first turkey with this still in it."

"Gross!" Nicole exclaimed.

Miguel laughed. "Inedible. So, what are you cooking this in?"

Jesse pulled a disposable aluminum-foil roasting pan from a bag under the table. Miguel double-checked the main cavity and arranged the turkey in the roaster, breast up. Then he inserted the thermometer and handed Jesse the baster. "That's it. Good luck."

"You're not going!" Jesse protested.

But he was. A moment later, he was gone. Jesse hesitantly put the turkey in the oven, then turned to Nicole. "Now what?"

"Don't look at me!"

"Can I help?" an amused voice asked from the

doorway. Charlie had gotten up out of his chair and maneuvered over in his walker.

"Charlie!" Jesse said. "I told you I had this under control."

Charlie chuckled. "You lied. Besides, I'm bored out there." He turned to Nicole. "I know how to cook those yams," he wheedled.

That settled it, as far as Nicole was concerned. "Get Charlie a chair," she told Jesse, clearing a spot at the table. Reluctantly Jesse set the old man up with a chair and moved his walker out to the hall.

"I can't see the game from here," Charlie said, pointing to the place he thought the TV should be moved to.

"It's only the stupid parade anyway," Jesse told him.

Charlie looked from him to Nicole and smiled. "We can switch back and forth now, can't we?"


"Shall we pray?" Mrs. del Rios asked.

Miguel and Rosa bowed their heads over plates loaded with macaroni casserole and salad. But just as they were about to begin, there was a knock at the door.

"Who can that be?" Mrs. del Rios asked, raising her eyes.

"I'll get it." Miguel had planned to get rid of whoever it was with record speed, but to his surprise, Jesse and Nicole stood on his doorstep.

"We brought back your stuff," Jesse said, handing him the baster and meat thermometer. With the other hand he held out a food-laden plate. "And we thought since your mom wasn't feeling up to cooking yet, maybe you guys could use some of this leftover turkey. Charlie will never get through all the leftovers we had."

"Yeah. Here's half a pie," Nicole added, forcing it on Miguel along with turkey. "It's chocolate cream. The pumpkin mix had an accident, so Charlie showed us how to make this instead." She leaned in closer. "Don't tell the pilgrims, but it's actually kind of better."

"You guys, we don't need this," Miguel protested, reluctant to take their charity.

But Jesse was insistent. "Please. Charlie will never eat it, and you can make sandwiches tomorrow if you don't want it for dinner."

It was easier to give in than to argue. "I'd invite you inside, but we were just sitting down. . . ."

"That's okay," Nicole said. "I have to get home anyway. Thank your mom for the tips on the turkey."

Miguel came back to the table with a heavy plate in each hand. "That was Jesse and Nicole. They brought us some turkey and pie."

"How nice!" his mother exclaimed. "How sweet of them to think of us."

"Yeah," said Miguel. "I guess.'"

"What do you mean, you guess? Put it down here." Mrs. del Rios cleared a spot in the center of the table.

"Ooh, that pie looks good," Rosa said, checking it out.

"*Now* let's say grace." Their mother composed herself, then began. "Father, we thank you for this food out of your bounty, and for the blessing of our friends. You've given us so much to be thankful for, it feels like Thanksgiving should last all year. And Father, we ask a special blessing for my kidney donor and his or her family. May you be with them in this difficult time, just as you are with us in our joy. In the name of the Father, the Son, and the Holy Spirit," she concluded, crossing herself as she spoke.

Miguel felt his spirits rise with the prayer. How could he be anything other than thankful on such an incredible day?

He helped himself to some turkey, thinking back to the night his mother had gone into surgery. It already seemed so long ago. He remembered his panicked pacing, his frantic prayers . . . it all seemed like a dream.

Except that his prayers had come true.

"Do you think the pilgrims were thankful for the Native Americans?" Amy asked, leaning forward across the breakfast bar. Her brown curls brushed the tiles.

"Huh? I don't know." Melanie was removing the feast Mrs. Murphy had prepared ahead of time from the oven where it had been heating. She set a hot mashed-potato casserole on the counter and went back for the sliced smoked turkey breast and yams.

"If they weren't, then why did they invent Thanksgiving?" Amy persisted.

"Well, they were probably pretty glad they hadn't frozen or starved to death yet. They were thankful for that."

"Yeah. But who were they giving thanks to? It's Thanks*giving*, right?"

Melanie shrugged, her hands still full. She'd never thought about it before. Of course, she'd never thought about most of the questions Amy had raised over the last twenty-four hours. The kid's mind never stopped.

"I kind of doubt they were thanking the Native Americans," Melanie said slowly.

But Amy had a point. They must have been thanking someone, so who? God. The answer stopped her halfway between the oven and the counter with a piping-hot tray of rolls in her hand. Was she right? She had to be—who else was there?

On the other hand, how had she managed to get through fifteen years of life without ever hearing that? She'd made the requisite paper-bag turkeys in grade school and colored all those cornucopias and dreary pilgrim scenes. And all she could remember hearing was that the pilgrims were giving thanks—for the harvest, for their survival. No one ever said *who* they were thanking.

"I think they must have been thanking God," she told Amy, the words awkward in her mouth.

Amy's eyes brightened. "That makes sense."

Melanie nodded and went to the dining room to get a tablecloth out of the china hutch. She and her father never used tablecloths—they never even used the formal dining room—but she wanted to make the occasion special for Amy. In the second drawer, near the bottom, she found a rich brown one. As she pulled it out, something fell from its folds and fluttered to the floor. Melanie set the cloth aside and picked up a greeting card.

HAPPY THANKSGIVING!

The words were emblazoned on top of an overflowing horn of plenty in bold black letters. Melanie opened the card as if in a dream, something tugging at the edges of her memory.

Inside it was blank, except for her mother's handwriting:

*Dearest Clay,*

*How can I be anything but thankful when I think of you and Mel? Happy Thanksgiving, sweetheart, and a lifetime of happy Thanksgivings to come.*

*All my love,*
*Tristyn*

"What is that?" Amy asked, reaching for the card.

Melanie pulled it back instinctively, not wanting it damaged. "A card my mother gave my father." How long ago it seemed now. Melanie checked for a date—she'd been ten that year.

"What's it doing in there?" Amy asked.

"I put it there, when Thanksgiving was over. We almost never use this stuff."

Melanie felt strange standing there holding that card, as if she were disturbing the dead somehow. When she had tucked it into the tablecloth, the possibility that her mother could die before any of them saw it again had been the furthest thing from her mind. At the time, her only thought had been that it would be fun for her mom to find again some future year, a happy reminder of the past. But with all the different tablecloths to choose from, she must have never run across it. And then the accident . . .

Melanie heard her father's footsteps at the top of the stairs. She threw the cloth over the table and quickly set three places, her father's at the head. Then, on an impulse, she stood the Thanksgiving card beside his water glass. Rushing back into the kitchen, she found him poking around the dishes.

"There you are, Mel! Boy, this smells good." He lifted the lid on a casserole and lurched closer.

He'd been drinking. It was clear to her, but she hoped Amy wouldn't notice. He was clean, he was dressed . . . a little girl might not pick up on it.

"Mrs. Murphy did herself proud," Melanie said tightly, grabbing the hot dish out from under him with a pair of pot holders. She carried it to the dining room, and moved the other food there as well. Then she took a bottle of apple cider from the refrigerator and went to pour them all drinks.

"Ooh, none of that for me, thanks," her father said, wandering into the dining room with a fresh beer in his hand. "After all, it is a holiday."

*A holiday from what?* Melanie thought bitterly as she helped Amy into her chair. *A holiday for who?* Ever since her mother had died, Melanie hated all the holidays. They were only reminders of what had been lost—reasons for her father to drink and for her to cry. She began scooping potatoes onto Amy's plate, resisting the tears she already felt burning in her eyes.

"What is this?"

The edge in her father's voice stopped her cold. He had picked up the card, opened it, and now he looked at her accusingly. "Where did you find this?"

"It was, uh, in the linens," she stammered. "I thought you'd like to see it again."

"Why?"

"Well, um . . ." Amy was watching, her eyes wide. "Mom wished you lots of happy Thanksgivings, that's all. I thought it was nice."

She glanced meaningfully down at Amy, then stared at her father, trying to telegraph with her eyes her desire not to have a scene.

He seemed to get it. Cautiously he set the card down at arm's length and picked up his beer instead. Melanie hurriedly scooped some potatoes onto his plate, then helped herself and Amy to thin slices of smoked turkey breast. The rest of the food was served equally quickly.

Melanie was nervously lifting the first bite to her mouth when Amy broke the silence. "Aren't we going to say grace?"

Melanie froze, then looked nervously toward her father. He still hadn't touched his fork, and his eyes were far away. Now, slowly, he turned them to Amy. "Sure, kid. Give it all you've got."

Amy nodded happily, unaware of the irony. She folded her small hands in front of her and earnestly closed her eyes.

"Dear God," she recited in a singsong tone. "We thank you for the food we eat; we thank you for the friends we meet. We thank you for your help each day, to live and learn and love and play. Amen." She dropped her hands and smiled radiantly. "My daddy taught me that one."

Melanie felt tears rising again. She chewed a piece of turkey and tried to swallow past the lump in her throat. She forced the food down somehow and took another bite.

"Hey, where's the cranberry sauce?" Amy demanded.

"Oops, I must have left it in the kitchen." Melanie jumped out of her seat, glad of an excuse to leave the table, even if only temporarily. The cranberries glittered in cut crystal on the kitchen counter, but Melanie didn't snatch them and go right back. Instead she grabbed the edge of the counter and squeezed, sucking in long deep breaths of cool air as she gazed out the windows overlooking the pool.

She'd been an idiot to leave that card out for her father. She should have known it would only upset him. And the timing . . . on a holiday, when he was already half drunk. How stupid could she be? A tear spilled down her cheek and she wiped it away angrily, determined it should be the last.

She knew what would happen now. He'd push the food around his plate for as long as his beer held out. He'd excuse himself before dessert. He'd disappear into his den. And then he'd drink until he passed out.

*Happy Thanksgiving, sweetheart,* Melanie thought sarcastically, wondering what her mother would make of all this.

She sucked in another deep breath and picked up the cranberry sauce. She would not cry. She wouldn't.

At least not until Amy was asleep.

# Nine

"Amen." Jenna concluded the Thanksgiving grace with a full heart, feeling incredibly lucky as she opened her eyes and looked around the table. All her sisters were there, including Mary Beth. The oldest Conrad girl had arrived barely an hour before, her curly hair a wild tangle around a freckled face flushed pink with the cold.

"I'm here!" she had bellowed from the doorway, stomping the feeling back into her feet after the long car ride. Jenna had run out with the others, then stopped in amazement—it was unbelievable how much Mary Beth and Maggie were starting to look alike.

"We should go around the table and say one thing we're thankful for," Mary Beth proposed now. "Mrs. Givens, you're the guest, so you should start."

The elderly neighbor the Conrads had invited to join them for dinner seemed taken aback for only a second. "Well, I'm thankful I have some mighty good neighbors, and for this delicious food in front of us."

Jenna smiled. Her family played this game every year, and it was considered poor form to count the food—too easy—but since Mrs. Givens was a guest they'd let her slide.

Maggie went next. "I'm thankful I'm in eighth grade now, and next year I'll be in high school. Then *everyone* will have to take me seriously."

Jenna wasn't sure what the hint was about, but her stomach lurched at the mere idea of being in the same school with Maggie.

"I'm thankful—incredibly thankful—for my new job," Caitlin said shyly.

Jenna's father was at the head of the table. "I'm thankful for the continued health of everyone here, and for all the things we've been able to enjoy together as a family." He said the same thing every year.

And then it was Jenna's turn. She aimed her remarks at Caitlin, who was sitting directly across the table. "I'm thankful for all my sisters. And I'm *especially* thankful that most of them still live at home."

She'd put too much emphasis on her words for them to pass without notice. As she'd hoped, Caitlin looked up at her, her expression surprised. Jenna knew what must be running through her sister's head: that Jenna had been the one who had wanted her to leave.

Jenna only smiled mysteriously, loving the secret she was keeping. Her plan was almost in place.

Soon Caitlin would know all about it. The thought broke her smile wide open.

She couldn't wait!

Leah dabbed instant glue on a final bead and used tweezers to position it on the inexpensive ceramic picture frame she was decorating. "Perfect," she breathed, pleased with the effect.

Picking up an official-looking envelope, she carefully removed the photograph that had arrived by mail the day before—her homecoming portrait with Miguel. Holding it delicately by the edges, she slipped the photo into the frame, then held it up to admire it.

The phone on her nightstand rang, startling her. She moved to her bed and snatched it up quickly, somehow sure who was on the other end. "Hello?"

"Hi, gorgeous," Miguel teased.

She smiled at the image of him she held in her hand. "You're going to say that to my mother someday," she warned, knowing how similar their voices were. "Personally, I can't wait, but *you* might find it embarrassing."

"I just called to say happy Thanksgiving. Put your mother on and I'll say it to her."

Leah set their photo on her nightstand, turning it back and forth to find the perfect angle. "I'd rather keep you all to myself."

The sigh at the other end of the line told her that her flirtation had found its mark. "I wish I could see you tonight," he said.

"Me too. I'll stop by tomorrow, though, after we finish shopping for the pancake breakfast."

"I feel bad about not helping with that."

"Don't. How many people does it take to buy some pancake mix and a few eggs? Melanie's not coming either, and she's only baby-sitting. How's your mother doing?"

"She's fine. That's the thing. I could go . . ."

"Will you forget it and just enjoy yourself for once? You're already going to be busy most of Saturday with the breakfast."

"Yeah. You're right." He paused. "Hey, you know what we talked about the other day?"

Leah wasn't sure what he meant, but she could tell by the sudden change in his voice that he'd come to the real reason for his call. "Refresh my memory."

"About me working at the hospital?"

"Oh. Yeah."

"Well, I think I want to do that. I've been thinking about it a lot. And I'm wondering, well . . . do you think I'd make a good doctor?"

"A doctor?"

"A surgeon, I mean. Because I was thinking, all this stuff with my mom . . . And I wonder now, if my dad had gone in earlier . . ." He took a deep breath and rushed ahead. "It's just that, now that my mom can work again, I feel like I have some breathing room. For now. Kidney transplants usually don't last forever, and down the road she could need another one. That could be ten or twenty years away, though, and if I were a doctor, I could really be there for her next time—in every way, not just financially."

Leah was overwhelmed, both by the unexpectedness of the idea and the unusual passion with which he'd just explained it. Still, the whole plan seemed so sudden. "I'm not sure it's a good idea to plan your career around helping your mother with another kidney transplant," she said gently. "You need to think about what *you* want to do, Miguel. For you. Because you can be there for her without being her doctor, but you're gong to be working at whatever you choose for the rest of your life."

There was a long, long pause. "You don't think I'd be good at it," he said at last.

"What? No! I think you'd be great. I only meant you should be sure it's what you want to do."

"It is. I mean . . . I think it is. This isn't just about my mother, Leah. Her surgery put it into my head— I won't deny that. But I saw a lot of other things, too, while I was at the hospital. I think I could make a difference there."

"I don't doubt it," she said, feeling herself go a little misty. He was so sincere, and the goal was so

129

enormous. She almost didn't know what to say. "I think you'd be terrific," she finally murmured.

"Thanks." Miguel was choked up too.

Leah's doorbell rang. "I have to go. My grand-parents are here for dinner. I'll see you tomorrow, okay?"

In the living room, Grandma and Grandpa Harris—her mother's parents—were still taking off their coats. Grandfather Rosenthal lived out of state and Leah rarely saw him. His wife, her father's mother, had died when Leah was so young that she knew her more from photographs than memory.

"Hi, Grandma. Grandpa," Leah said, running up to give them both a kiss. "Is it cold outside?"

Her grandfather shrugged. "Cold enough, I reckon. Be snowing soon if this keeps up."

"We'll heat you up," Leah's dad promised them. "Arlene's got a batch of curry in there that would peel the paint off a barn."

"I don't know what's so awful about turkey," Grandma Harris whispered wistfully to Leah. "Just once . . ."

Leah smiled. Her mom had an aversion to cook-ing the traditional American dinner—boring, she called it. So every year was a new adventure. This year it was Indian food.

Mrs. Rosenthal came out of the kitchen with a tray of fancy appetizers and a steaming pot of exotic-smelling tea. She set it all down on the coffee table and hugged her parents.

"Who was on the phone?" she asked as everyone gathered around to try the hors d'oeuvres.

Leah had just bitten into something like a miniature vegetable turnover. "Miguel," she answered eagerly, despite her full mouth. "His mom is doing great with her new kidney and now he's thinking of becoming a doctor."

"A doctor!" Leah's grandmother exclaimed. "Well, that's just fine. More young people need to set their sights high."

"A doctor," Leah's father repeated. "Does he know you have to go to college for that?" But he was kidding. Now that they understood Miguel's situation, Leah's parents were embarrassed about the way they'd acted when he'd revealed his plan to work straight out of high school.

"Very funny," Leah said breezily. "I'll tell him you wish him outrageous success."

She was only teasing, but, to her surprise, her mother reached across the table and laid a hand on her arm. "Do that," she urged. "Really."

Leah looked from her mother to her father. He seemed embarrassed, but nodded agreement.

"Who's this Miguel?" Grandpa Harris broke in grumpily, as if they were all keeping secrets.

"Why, he's Leah's young man, dear. Pay more attention."

Leah smiled happily. Her young man! She couldn't wait to tell Miguel that one.

Jesse had his hand on the car door handle even before Dr. Jones's silver Mercedes pulled into the garage. The moment it stopped, he leapt out, leaving his father, stepmother, and stepsister still fumbling with their seat belts.

"I'm going to bed," he announced in a voice that dared them to argue. No one did, even though it was barely nine o'clock.

*They're probably as sick of me as I am of them*, Jesse thought, hurrying through the house to the staircase. He ran up the stairs to his room and slammed the door behind him.

Dinner had been a total drag. He ripped off his necktie and threw it on the floor in disgust. It had been Elsa's idea to eat at a restaurant—heaven forbid that his self-involved stepmother should risk breaking a nail by cooking a turkey like every other mother in Missouri. No, better they should all put on their least comfortable clothes and eat a late supper at the phoniest restaurant in town. Jesse peeled off his sports coat and dropped it next to the tie.

The whole thing had made him sick: Elsa decked out like it was prom night; Brittany simpering in a new white dress; his father in a black suit, acting like Don Juan to Elsa, Santa Claus to Brittany, and the Grinch to Jesse. Ever since Jesse had gotten suspended from school, Dr. Jones had been coolly aloof. The man seemed to have no concept of when his point had already been made.

Jesse walked blindly across his bedroom and sat on his unmade bed. Overcooked beans and half-burned rolls at Charlie's had tasted better than gourmet fare with the enemy. He couldn't help remembering other Thanksgivings.

*Better Thanksgivings . . .*

On an impulse, he picked up the phone and dialed his mother in California. It was two hours earlier there. But after the phone rang three or four times, an answering machine picked up.

"Hi, this is Beth. I can't take your call right now . . ."

Jesse's heart leapt at the sound of his mother's voice, but fell as soon as he realized it was a recording. He tried to decide whether or not to leave a message. It was possible she was home, screening calls, in which case she'd be sure to pick up if he said it was him. But it was equally possible someone had invited her to their house, now that she was living alone. If he left a message and she wasn't home, she'd have to call him back later. His mother almost never called, for fear his dad or Elsa would answer.

"Please wait for the tone before you begin and—"

Jesse hung up quickly. He wanted to talk to her

now, not spend the next twenty-four hours wondering when she was going to call back. Besides, he hated leaving messages. People invariably returned his calls ten minutes after he'd decided he didn't want to talk to them anymore.

He fell back onto his pillows and kicked off his shoes. Unbuckling his belt, he pulled it through the loops without getting up, then unbuttoned his collar and cuffs. *I should do something*, he thought, staring up at the ceiling. But it was a random thought. He had no idea what he'd meant by it.

His mind wandered back to his mother, then to his two brothers, away at college. Downstairs, Elsa's high, artificial laughter rang out, piercing enough to annoy him even from such a distance. Jesse felt his body sink farther into the bed, and even though the lights were still on, the room seemed a little darker. He closed his eyes and went with it. Sinking . . . sinking . . . he desperately needed a drink.

He sat up abruptly, disoriented by the sudden brightness. Switching on a tiny reading lamp next to his bed, he got up and turned off the overhead light. He hesitated with his ear to his closed door for a second; then he moved to the closet and silently opened it. On the shelf, in the back, wrapped in a seldom-worn sweater, he found what he was looking for.

The nearly empty vodka bottle glittered as Jesse brought it to his bed and flopped down on the mattress. There were only two inches of liquid left, but two inches were enough—enough to take the edge off, anyway.

He stared into the bottle as though he could read his future there. And suddenly he thought of Charlie. Charlie the alcoholic, who hadn't touched a drink in fifteen years. Jesse tried to imagine keeping the liquor he was holding around that long, untouched, but he couldn't. He was only a year older than fifteen himself.

With a quick, determined twist of the cap, he sat up and tossed back the bottle's entire contents, not breathing while he swallowed. The liquor went down easier that way, he'd found. It burned less. He pulled off his dress shirt, wrapped it around the empty bottle, and chucked it under the bed to dispose of later. Then he collapsed onto his pillows and switched off the reading light.

Moonlight shone in from outside. Jesse pulled a quilt over his bare chest, even though the warmth in his belly was already starting to spread. The longed-for haziness was taking over his senses. He was drifting, floating . . . better. So much better.

His mind skipped from thought to thought. From his mother to his father to the state finals game the next night. All those things seemed far away, though. Comfortably removed. On Saturday he'd go to the pancake breakfast with Eight Prime. Maybe he'd try to work next to Melanie. Melanie . . .

He could feel himself falling asleep. He tried to fight it, hating to waste the buzz, the delicious sensation that the bed wasn't solid beneath him. But he was so tired all of a sudden, so comfortable. Just before he drifted off, his mind returned to Charlie.

*I wonder how a guy knows when he's an alcoholic?*

# Ten

"No! No, do it like this!" Amy cried, her shrill, excited voice carrying over the noise in the crowded mall. She demonstrated her best duckwalk for Tanya Jeffries's eight-year-old twin brothers, stepping out well in front of Melanie and Tanya. The boys shrugged and fell in behind her, the three of them quacking like ducks with an attitude.

"I don't think Amy's feeling shy anymore," Melanie said to her friend from the cheerleading squad. "She seems to have decided your brothers are all right."

Tanya nodded. "I don't know how we're going to get any shopping done with those three. After-Thanksgiving sales only save you money if you dare actually enter the store." The width of her smile made it clear she didn't really mind, though. Melanie knew Tanya was devoted to her brothers, even more so now that her parents had finally concluded an ugly divorce. The boys *were* adorable, in their basketball sneakers and matching denim overalls, their black hair shaved close to their heads. Between them they had more long, thick lashes than four mascara commercials.

"It's such a waste on boys," Tanya had sighed, even though she'd made out all right in the eyelashes department herself.

At first Amy had seemed a little afraid of the twins. After all, there were two of them, and they were bigger and older than she was. But it hadn't taken her long to decide they were okay, and now she was running the show.

"No, like this!" she insisted. "Quack . . . *quack*."

Bryan and Bayley answered with quacks unchanged in the slightest.

"Yes!" said Amy, beaming proudly.

"All right, that's enough quacking." Tanya motioned the kids back to her. "There are too many people in here for that now."

She was right—the mall was becoming more packed by the minute. The boys drifted back and took their sister's hands, one on each side, and Melanie felt an unexpected longing pierce her heart. She grabbed Amy's hand to counter it, but she knew it wasn't the same. Amy wasn't her sister, however much she might like to pretend she was. They didn't even live together. The weekend would pass, Amy would go home . . . and Tanya would still have her brothers.

"Tawn, you said you'd buy us something if we were good," Bryan reminded her.

"That's right. *If* you were good."

"Well, we haven't been bad," Bayley reasoned.

Tanya smiled down at them. "The morning's still young. I'm not buying you two anything until we're on our way out the door."

"Aw, Tawn," they said in unison, leaning their heads against her. They walked like that for a while, all three taking comfort from the contact.

Melanie had never much regretted being an only child before, but she did at that moment. Watching the way the twins trusted Tanya suddenly made her feel even more alone. She would never have a brother or sister of her own—just one more anchor she'd been denied, something she could have held on to. . . .

She squeezed Amy's hand hard. It wasn't the same.

Nicole wandered through the door of the bulk-quantity warehouse behind Peter and Jenna, dazed by the food stacked up to the ceiling. Food! After eating two Thanksgiving dinners the day before, Nicole never wanted to see food again. Her hand moved self-consciously to her stomach, pressing the flesh through her sweater. The scale said she'd only gained a pound, but Nicole didn't believe it—it felt like she'd swallowed a basketball.

"What's the first thing on the list?" Ben asked, pressing up eagerly beside her.

Jenna checked the sheet of paper in her hand. "Orange juice."

"I'll get that!" He started to dash off, his sneakers squeaking on the concrete floor.

"No, Ben!" Leah stopped him. "Let's not buy stuff in the order of the list. Let's follow the order of the store. Here." She grabbed the handle of a low rolling platform—the warehouse equivalent of a grocery cart—and began to push it in his direction.

"Uh, I'll get that," Peter said quickly, stepping forward to intercept the cart.

Nicole could imagine what he was thinking—letting clumsy Ben steer something that heavy and hard to turn could end in a vehicular manslaughter.

"No, let me." Jesse took the handle from Peter. "I don't feel like thinking today. I'll push the cart if you guys load it up."

The group of six began moving down the first aisle, eyes peeled for anything that might be on their list. Jesse brought up the rear, and Nicole drifted back to walk next to him. He seemed distracted, maybe even a little down.

"So what's the story?" she asked. "Worried about the game tonight?"

He shrugged. "I think we'll win," he said, with a marked lack of enthusiasm.

"Sure we will! Of course!"

Jesse barely smiled.

"Here," Leah said, putting two bags of ground coffee, one regular, one decaf, on the platform.

Ben set a box of stirring sticks beside it. Cream and sugar followed before the group began moving again.

At the end of the aisle, a harried-looking woman in an apron was handing out pizza egg rolls. Nicole's stomach rumbled hungrily at the spicy aroma, but she ignored it. There was no way she was eating one.

"Thanks anyway," she said, waving off the free sample.

Jesse wrestled the cart through a U-turn. "I'll take hers," he said. He grabbed two as he passed by on the straightaway, popping one into his mouth as he and Nicole walked down the next aisle. "I can't believe you're passing this up," he said, holding the other one under her nose. "They're free and they're good."

Nicole's mouth watered, but she turned her head. "Do you have any idea how much I ate yesterday? All day long it was 'Eat this, Nicole' and 'Try that, Nicole.' I'm not eating again before Monday, at the earliest." She had expected approving support, but Jesse only jerked his head impatiently.

"What are you talking about? You hardly ate anything at Charlie's."

"Yes, I did!" she protested. "I ate turkey and . . ."

She was about to list every bite of food she'd consumed—both then and later—when she suddenly realized it might not be wise to provide much

141

detail. People just wanted to see the end result; they didn't want to hear about the hard work that went into it. She drew herself up a little taller, content with the knowledge that, despite the pound she'd gained, she was still nearly as thin as a magazine model.

"You ought to eat more anyway," Jesse said, polishing off the second pizza roll. "You're getting too skinny."

The smile that broke out on her face was so wide it hurt. Jesse had just given her the ultimate compliment. Her chest pulled up a little, her shoulders went back. And then something horrible happened—she looked into his eyes and realized he was *serious*.

"You *can't* get too skinny," she objected, shocked.

"Yeah, you can. You should take a page from Jenna. Jenna has the right idea."

He nodded toward Jenna, up near the front of the group. She had been nibbling cautiously at her hot pizza roll, but as Nicole watched she popped the final bite into her mouth, licking her fingers with relish.

"*Jenna?*" Nicole squeaked, doubly shocked. "Don't you think Jenna's a little, well . . . chunky?" She whispered the awful final word, terrified of being overheard.

Jesse stared as if she were crazy. "No way. Jenna enjoys herself—Jenna's real. I like the way she looks."

"You do?"

He nodded, a little spark of life finally creeping into his eyes. "You think she and Peter have something going on?"

"Why? Are you interested?"

Jesse made a face. "Not like that. Geez, Nicole. I was only trying to have a conversation."

"Oh. Right."

Having conversations—that was what friends did.


"This is not looking good," Tanya whispered to Melanie.

The cheerleaders were lined up along the edge of the frigid field, their feet shoulder width apart, their red-knuckled hands on their hips. In front of them the Wildcats battled Marshton and behind them a huge crowd filled the bleachers. In this fourth quarter of the first state finals game, however, the atmosphere had turned more funereal than celebratory. The Wildcats were getting pounded, despite their home-field advantage.

"You're right," Melanie mouthed back. She felt disloyal saying so, but CCHS's football season had clearly come to an end.

"Let's go! Wildcat Spirit!" Vanessa shouted, calling another cheer. The squad turned to face the bleachers and began walking through the yell, nearly as dazed as the team seemed to be. Every motion was sharp, every pattern precise—Sandra had them at the top of their form—but there was a desperate edge to their voices as they tried to rally the crowd.

The dream was over. Everybody knew it.

A few minutes later it was official. The people who had driven in from Marshton erupted in a frenzy of cheering. Helmets were tossed into the air, players were lifted onto shoulders—but not on the Wildcats' side of the field. The CCHS players filed off the grass, stunned, muddy, and beaten, while their teammates on the bench threw towels over their heads so no one would see their tears of disappointment.

The cheerleaders were crying too. Seniors Vanessa and Tiffany were bawling on each other's shoulders, and all the other girls' faces reflected varying degrees of tragedy. Tenderhearted Angela was a mess, and even Tanya was sniffling. Melanie felt a tear slide down her own cold cheek, but she quickly wiped it away, annoyed to show weakness over something so stupid. A few quick, deep breaths and she had herself back in control.

And then she caught sight of Jesse, head down like the others, walking toward the locker room. The 89 on his jersey was half hidden by mud, and one shoulder seam was ripped. Without a word to her sobbing squad leader, Melanie ran to catch up.

"You played really well," she said, knowing how hard he'd be taking the defeat. "It's not your fault we lost."

He just shrugged and kept walking. She put out a

hand to stop him, resting it on his arm. "I know it's tough, but look on the bright side—at least we got into the finals this year."

Jesse's annoyed shake of the head made it clear he had no intention of looking on the bright side, and Melanie had to wonder why she'd felt compelled to play Pollyanna.

"I just—I wanted to make sure you were okay," she said awkwardly. "I mean, I know you're fine, but . . . you know."

Jesse's angry look made her flush in spite of the freezing air.

"No. I'm not okay," he spit. "I'm far from okay. So why don't you run back to your little girlfriends or go kiss up to Peter and leave me the hell alone."

She might have returned his rudeness if it hadn't been for something around his eyes. Something so wild, so lost, it made her wonder if he even knew what he was saying.

He jerked his arm away from her hand. "I mean it, Melanie. Leave."

"All right," she said slowly, backing off. "But I'll see you tomorrow at the pancake breakfast. You're still coming, right?"

His laugh was loud and humorless. "Oh, sure. Wait for me. Hold your breath until I get there."

Melanie's temper flared at last. "Look, I'm sorry you guys didn't win, but don't take it out on me. What's the matter with you, anyway?"

"I just . . ." Tears brimmed in his cool blue eyes. "Without football, there's nothing, all right? Without football, *I'm* nothing. I don't even know how I'll survive till next year."

His words took her by surprise. They scared her a little too. She opened her mouth to argue, but he was already running off. She watched helplessly as he disappeared into the crowd, his shoulders impossibly wide in their game-day pads, his hips slender and strong.

*He didn't mean he wouldn't survive,* Melanie tried to reassure herself. *He's just upset and he's talking crazy.* But she wasn't reassured.

"Melanie!" a happy voice cried behind her. Amy's arms wrapped around her bare legs, dragging her down toward the grass. "Melanie, I got you!"

"You sure do." Melanie turned around in Amy's bear hug and gently disentangled herself. "What did you do with Peter and Jenna? You didn't ditch them, did you?"

Amy laughed delightedly, as if she'd love to get up to such mischief. "No. They're coming."

A moment later, Melanie saw Peter's blond head rising above the crowd on the field. Taking Amy's hand, she went to meet him and Jenna halfway.

"Hi. Thanks for watching her," Melanie said.

"Are you kidding?" Peter reached down to muss Amy's brown curls affectionately. "Amy's our buddy!"

Amy squirmed happily but didn't relax her grip

146

on Melanie. Melanie smiled at her, grateful for the show of favoritism, but when she looked back up she noticed something new—something that made every other bad thing that had happened that night seem minor in comparison.

Peter and Jenna were holding hands.

# Eleven

Miguel approached the door of the church hall a little tentatively, Leah at his side. It was early—so early that the sky was still dark and the birds weren't yet singing—and the late November chill nipped purposefully at his nose. He knew it wouldn't be much longer before the first snowflakes of the season dusted the ground like sugar. But in spite of the appallingly early hour, in spite of the pervasive cold, even in spite of the fact that he was going to spend all morning working his butt off, Miguel was in a good mood. No, Miguel was in a great mood.

"Do you know what today is?" he asked Leah, pushing a heavy glass door open. A welcome blast of warm air hit them in the face as they made their way inside.

"Uh . . . Saturday?" she ventured, an uncomprehending smile on her face.

"That's right! It's Saturday!"

She shook her head, still not getting it.

"It's dialysis day! Dialysis every Saturday for the

last two years—and now I'm finally free!" He thought of his mother and Rosa, still snug in their beds at home. "We're all free," he added gratefully. "I can't believe I'm here."

Leah slipped her hand into his. "Saturday mornings are definitely looking up all the way around," she teased, smiling as her eyes locked with his. "It's a big improvement from my perspective too."

For a moment, he considered kissing her. There was no one around to see them. The room they were standing in was a masterpiece of precisely arranged tables and chairs, but the lights were only halfway on and the only people there were—

*Crash! CRASH!*

"Ben!" Jenna wailed in the distance, her voice muffled by the closed door of an adjacent room.

Leah burst into giggles at her friend's distraught tone. The moment for kissing was shattered.

"I'm guessing it's this way to the kitchen," Miguel laughed, heading in the direction of the ruckus.

"No, Amy, sweetie, let somebody big do that." Melanie rushed to remove a large cardboard flat of eggs from the little girl's hands.

"I'm only taking them to Peter," Amy protested in an injured voice.

"Let her do it," Nicole muttered. "It's safer than letting Ben."

"Ah, but Ben is more efficient," Leah joked. "By

the time he gets to Peter, half the eggs are already broken."

Nicole rolled her eyes. "Yeah. Who needs to scramble them? Just put them through a strainer."

Melanie took the eggs from Amy anyway, shooting a glance at Ben to make sure he hadn't overheard. But Ben was on the far side of the kitchen, next to the pass-through for the drinks, oblivious to everything but the giant coffee percolator a lady named Maya was explaining to him.

She carried the eggs to Peter, past the flat silver griddles where Jesse and Miguel were precooking the sausage links, browning them till they were nearly done. Their spicy aroma permeated the kitchen, overpowering even the sharp scent of citrus from the oranges Nicole and Leah were cutting into paper-thin slices to garnish the plates.

"Here's more eggs." Melanie set them on the counter beside Peter, deliberately turning her back on Jesse as she did so. He had finally shown up, late and hung over. Not that he'd told anyone he'd been drinking, of course. He didn't need to—Melanie considered herself an expert in hangover recognition. Since then he'd been hanging out behind the griddle, speaking only when he absolutely had to. *The smell of these sausages must be turning his stomach*, she thought with a certain satisfaction.

"Thanks." Peter was breaking eggs into an enormous steel bowl, an expression of deep concentration on his face.

Jenna stirred pancake batter in a matching bowl on his other side. "How's this, Melanie?" she asked, peering down into it. "Do you think it's supposed to be absolutely smooth? Or should I leave it lumpy, like muffins?"

Melanie only stared. Not only didn't she know, every time she looked at Jenna now, all she could see was her friend's hand enveloped in Peter's at the game the night before. She wanted badly to believe the incident had meant nothing, but her heart told her something else.

A white-haired woman moved in quickly from a few feet away. "Make it smooth, dear," she advised, "and not too thick, either. We're going to be pouring it out of a pitcher." She added some water to the bowl and motioned for Jenna to keep whisking before she moved off again.

"Thanks, Mrs. Howard," Jenna called after her. "It's so great having the Boosters here to help us," she told Melanie. "With their help, I feel like we can't go wrong."

With an effort, Melanie forced her wandering thoughts back to the pancake breakfast. She wasn't quite as sanguine about their success as Jenna, but as she gazed around the huge kitchen, she had to admit that things were pretty well under control.

The sausages filled two silver tubs beside two griddles, and two more griddles were heating up to cook the pancakes and eggs. Despite Ben's assistance, the Boosters had succeeded in mixing the frozen orange juice and setting out full cups to be picked up by diners with loaded plates. A plastic tub of iced individual milk cartons had been set next to the juice. All that remained was to cook the scrambled eggs and pancakes. Then people could start lining up to be served.

The swinging door to the hall popped open abruptly. "Are we ready?" Chris Hobart asked. He was a college student and Peter's partner in the Junior Explorers. "People are backing up out here, and we're going to start letting them in."

"I guess so." Peter looked questioningly at one of the Boosters, who nodded. "Yeah, start letting them in." Carrying his bowl of beaten eggs to a griddle, Peter poured some onto the hot surface. The eggs turned opaque immediately, bubbling up almost faster than Peter could scramble them. He slashed at the mixture with a spatula, trying to chop it up. Maya rushed over and turned down the heat.

"Come on, Jenna," Chris called anxiously. "Better start the pancakes."

"What do you want me and Amy to do?" Melanie asked Peter. He was still scrambling frantically, but Maya had added more liquid and his work was starting to resemble eggs.

"You, Leah, and Nicole are going be serving, right? You'd better send Amy to hang out with Chris and the rest of the Junior Explorers."

"I want to help!" Amy whined.

"Then help me," Chris told her, taking her hand. "You can pass out the plates when people buy their tickets."

Amy looked somewhat mollified as Chris hustled her into the hall. The swinging kitchen door let in a burst of noise as they left. People were already crowding in from outside, their voices clashing and combining as they greeted one another. Then the adult volunteers began opening all the pass-throughs from the kitchen into the main room, and the chatter and cries of "Good morning" turned into a constant dull roar.

"We've got coffee! We've got coffee!" Ben shouted excitedly, his voice carrying over everything.

"Alert the media," Jesse grumbled. The sausages were sizzling again.

Leah and Nicole walked by and set two bowls of orange garnishes near the end of the serving counter. The plan was to bring batches of food forward as they were cooked, with the three girls loading the food onto plates before it could get cold—one girl on pancakes, one on eggs, and one on sausage.

"I've got sausage ready!" Miguel called out.

Leah hurried over to take a tub full of links and a set of serving tongs.

"Eggs any second," Peter called. "Boy, these cook fast." He began scraping up scrambled eggs with his spatula, dropping them into another serving tub.

"Slow down, you guys!" Jenna squealed beside him. "I don't have any pancakes yet."

"We should use two griddles for pancakes and only one for sausage," Melanie suggested as she picked up the first batch of eggs. "The sausages are almost cooked now anyway, and pancakes take up a lot more room."

"Exactly," Mrs. Howard cut in. She tossed Jesse a clean, wet towel. "Let that other young man take over the sausage now, and wipe down your griddle with that. We need you on pancake duty."

"Pancake duty!" Jesse repeated sarcastically. "Gee, I hope I can handle it."

Melanie felt her lips purse into a tight little O. One of these days, someone was going to lose their sense of humor and whack Jesse upside the head.

*Oh wait*, she thought, smiling a little. *I already did that*.


"Well, what do you think?" Jenna asked happily, filling her father's coffee cup. "I think it's going well."

"Very well," both parents agreed.

All around the hall, the tables were filled nearly to capacity, and there were still people lining up to be fed. Jenna had already cooked so many pancakes, she'd lost track, but Maya had traded jobs with her for a few minutes to give Jenna a chance to talk to her family. All the Conrads were there, from Mary Beth right down to Sarah.

"Who cooked the pancakes?" Maggie demanded. "Mine were burned."

"They were not!" Jenna exclaimed, horrified.

Both Maggie and Mary Beth burst into boisterous laughter, causing heads to turn down the length of the table.

"We're just joshing you, Jenna," said Mary Beth. "I told her to say that."

Jenna forced a small, twisted smile to her lips. *Just what Maggie needs*, she thought. *More help being obnoxious.*

It was impossible to hold a grudge on such a beautiful day, though, and a moment later Jenna had forgotten the whole incident. She moved on to pour more coffee, noticing how the sunshine streaming though the windows created shifting patterns of light across the tabletops and worn blue carpeting and lit the smiles of the parishioners. Down at the end of the room, the table occupied by the Junior Explorers suddenly burst into song.

"*Oh, they built the ship* Titanic *to sail the ocean blue . . .*"

It was one of the songs Jenna had taught the kids around the campfire the previous summer. Chris hushed them before they could start pounding the table in time to the beat, but not before Jenna caught their eyes and smiled.

*This year the kids will be going to camp in a brand-new bus—and a good one too*, she thought happily. Looking around at all the support in the room, Jenna had never been more sure of anything in her life.

Afternoon shadows were creeping across the carpet by the time Eight Prime was nearly ready to go home. Leah leaned back in a folding chair, exhausted. The kitchen was finally clean, and everyone had gathered at one of the dining tables to count their earnings.

"I never knew breakfast could last so long," she moaned, rubbing a sore muscle in her neck. Between the prep time beforehand and the cleanup afterward, they'd been working longer than seven hours.

"You're not lying," Jesse said, raising his head. He'd been resting it on the table, more asleep than awake.

Leah smiled at him, glad he was snapping out of the funk he'd been in all morning. She knew losing the game the night before had been hard on him, although none of them had mentioned it. Eight Prime had been in unanimous, if silent, agreement on that point.

Miguel reached over to rub her neck with one strong hand. "So, Nicole, how much did we make?"

"Hang on," Nicole replied, tallying her columns. She always drew out her announcements, milking the moments for all they were worth.

"One thousand, two hundred and nine dollars," she said at last. "And that's after subtracting for the carpet guy to clean up Ben's big coffee stain."

"That could have happened to anyone!" Ben said. "Maya shouldn't have left that pot so close to the edge."

"Of course not—I don't know what she was thinking," Nicole returned sarcastically. "Setting down the coffeepot on the coffee table and all."

They were tired, and there might have been more arguing if Jenna hadn't interceded. "We know it wasn't your fault, Ben," she said quickly, laying one hand on his arm. "It was just an accident."

Ben raised his chin a little. "I don't know why we have to call it *my* stain then."

"Let's talk about the bus," Melanie suggested. Amy was falling asleep on her lap; the rest of the Junior Explorers had already gone home.

"Good idea." Peter glanced over Nicole's figures, then checked them against his own. "If we add what we made today to what we already had, we've got ten thousand, seventy-three dollars and twenty-five cents."

Nicole heaved a weary sigh. "That means we're still barely halfway there."

"Yeah, if we insist on buying the most expensive bus in town," Jesse said. "We could buy one tomorrow if we lowered our sights a little."

"I don't *want* to lower my sights," Melanie said, gazing at him over the top of Amy's brown head. "We already agreed we weren't going to buy a junky bus."

Jesse shrugged and looked out the window.

"We have to face the possibility that we might not get the bus Mr. Haig found for us, though," Leah said. "We only have half the money, and who knows how long that private school will wait before they decide they have to sell it? If they put an ad in the newspaper, we're probably going to lose it."

Peter nodded. "You're right, but I'm not giving up. If that's the bus God wants us to have, I know we'll get it somehow."

Leah's eyes widened. She knew Peter believed in God, but did he honestly believe an all-powerful deity would spend time on something as insignificant as a school bus?

A moment later she shook her head. She knew Peter did believe that.

In a way, she really envied him.

"So, uh, Courtney said you go to private school," Nicole ventured, trying to force her blind date into some sort of conversation. He'd introduced himself as Guy Vaughn when Courtney and

Jeff had picked her up, but once they'd backed out of the Brewsters' driveway, Courtney had started yakking away to Jeff, and Guy had become completely silent.

"That's right. Ozarks Prep. Ever heard of it?"

She'd heard of it. Ozarks Prep was a big-time Christian school—not one of those superficially religious academies where everyone pretended it was all about academics. No wonder Courtney had such a problem with him. Even Nicole was taken aback.

"Oh. Uh, do you like it there?" she asked, giving him a closer look.

He seemed normal enough: reddish brown hair, unremarkable features, a plain blue crew-necked sweater. . . . He didn't *look* like a fanatic.

"Of course. It's a great school." He seemed surprised she would even ask.

Nicole leaned forward and gripped the back of Courtney's seat, eager to change the subject. "So what movie are we going to?"

"*Born to Die*," Courtney said immediately. "Bill Glass said it was the scariest movie he ever saw."

"Sounds good to me," Nicole agreed.

"Isn't that a horror movie?" Guy asked.

Nicole saw her friend's shoulders tense. Courtney turned around slowly, a counterfeit smile on her lips. "Do you have a problem with that?"

"Well . . . yeah. I don't want to watch that junk; do you?"

"Apparently."

"We can see that anytime, Courtney," Jeff said quickly. "Let's go to a movie everyone likes."

Courtney turned back around in her seat. "I don't think *Tinkerbell* is playing," she muttered.

Nicole hoped she was the only one who had heard her.

By the time they had parked at the mall and started walking to the triplex, nobody was talking. Jeff and Guy were quiet by choice, Courtney was sulking, and Nicole didn't know what to say. She lagged a step behind Courtney and Jeff as they approached the ticket window—next to Guy, but not with him.

"Oh, great," Courtney groaned. "There's nothing else playing."

"What are you talking about?" Jeff asked. "There's *My Father the Firefly* and *Too Many Puppies*."

"*That's* what I'm talking about!" Courtney turned her back on the marquee and crossed her arms under her full bust. "A geek-fest and a cartoon."

"I vote for the cartoon," Guy said without missing a beat. "I've heard it's really funny."

Jeff put a hand on Courtney's shoulder. "Yes, let's see *Too Many Puppies*."

Courtney shrugged his hand off angrily and moved a few steps away. "Whatever." .

In the theater, Courtney made the guys sit in the

outside seats so that she and Nicole were together in the middle. "Can you believe this hokey crap?" she whispered over the huge tub of popcorn she had purchased. "If anyone sees us, I'll die."

"If anyone sees us, they'll be watching *Too Many Puppies* too," Nicole pointed out, only slightly less embarrassed than her friend. "They'd be ratting us out at their peril."

Courtney giggled. Nicole plunged her hand into the popcorn, spilling kernels all over Courtney's lap. Courtney flicked one back at Nicole and hit her in the arm. It wasn't even funny, but they both laughed harder than ever.

Then Jeff whispered something to Courtney, and Courtney began whispering back, jabbing the air with one finger for emphasis.

Abandoned, Nicole turned reluctantly toward her date. "Popcorn?"

One corner of his upper lip rose slightly as his eyes traveled to the mess she had made. "No, thank you. Look, the movie's starting." He inclined his head slightly toward the screen, as if she couldn't figure that out for herself.

Courtney poked her in the ribs from the other side.

"Ow!" Nicole giggled, wheeling around. "What's that for?"

"Ooh, too many puppies—I'm scared!" Courtney whimpered.

"I'll be right here," Nicole lectured in her best

161

imitation of her mother. "If it gets too scary, you can always hold my hand."

Courtney grabbed her hand and squeezed it so hard Nicole's knuckles cracked. Nicole jerked it back and the two of them burst into laughter again. Somewhere in the middle of the giggles, Nicole glanced guiltily at Guy, but he was staring stone-faced at the screen, as if she weren't even there. She turned back to her best friend.

"Jeff says we're acting like a couple of little kids," Courtney informed her.

Nicole rolled her eyes. "Then we ought to fit right in."

She *felt* like a kid, sitting in that theater full of children, watching a full-length cartoon. Not that she'd particularly wanted to see Courtney's slasher movie, either, but someone could have planned a little better. She glanced at Guy again, who seemed totally engrossed, and noticed his nose was Roman—a smooth, curved line.

Eventually she and Courtney settled down, mostly because they'd run out of snide comments and their cheeks hurt from smiling so much. The movie ran its predictable course, and by the time every last cartoon puppy had found a blissfully happy home, Nicole felt more like sleeping than laughing. She'd been up at the crack of dawn to help with the pancake breakfast, not to mention all the hours she'd worked, and she was running out of steam. She sur- reptitiously stifled a yawn as the four of them stood up. She didn't want the others to think she was some sort of baby, up past her bedtime, and she didn't want to mention Eight Prime in front of Guy. They filed out of the theater and through the lobby, then paused at the glass exit doors.

"Should we get some ice cream or something?" Jeff asked. "It's still pretty early."

Nicole glanced anxiously at Courtney. The en- tire weekend was turning into a feeding frenzy, and the last thing she needed was ice cream. To her re- lief, Courtney vetoed the idea.

"I'm sorry, but I'm really tired," she said, unable to keep from looking at Guy. "I think I ought to be getting home."

There was no doubt in Nicole's mind what her friend was thinking. She'd convince Jeff to drop off Guy and Nicole, and then, when she and Jeff were alone, she'd miraculously find a second wind. That was fine with Nicole. The evening couldn't end too soon, as far as she was concerned.

In the car on the way home, though, she started wondering if she'd given Guy a fair chance. He really wasn't that bad looking, and, aside from go- ing to Ozarks Prep, he seemed reasonably normal. The fact that Courtney couldn't stand the guy wasn't much of an indicator. She hated Peter and

Jenna, too, and she *really* hated it when Jeff wanted to hang out with them.

*Court's probably afraid Jeff is going to catch religion and try to ram it down her throat,* Nicole thought. She glanced at the back of Jeff's immaculately combed black hair. *Good luck,* she told him silently.

"So, Guy," she said, turning her attention to her date, "what did you think of the movie?" It was lame, but it was all she could think of.

He seemed to appreciate the effort anyway. "It was all right. I'll bet my little brother would really like it."

"You have a brother? How old?"

"Kenny's eight. I have a sister, too. Brenda's thirteen, but she's going through a stage right now where she thinks she's incredibly sophisticated."

"Tell me about it!" Nicole said. "I have a thirteen-year-old sister too, so I know what pains in the butt they are."

"I didn't say she was a pain. Maybe just a little full of herself."

"A little!" Nicole snorted. She moved closer to Guy on the broad backseat. "You're a junior, right? What's your favorite class?"

He looked her over carefully before he answered, but Nicole had no idea why. "Math, I guess. I like them all."

"Oh, I'm just horrible at math," she said flirtatiously, widening her eyes so he could see how clear and blue they were. "I think most girls are."

"That's a stereotype. The best student in my class is a girl." He was so deadly serious, he didn't even seem to realize she'd been trying to flirt with him. "You shouldn't buy into such generalizations. They'll only hold you back."

Nicole smiled insincerely. The guy was truly as boring as Courtney had promised.

*Oh well, I gave it my best shot*, she thought, facing forward in her seat. *No one can say I wasn't nice.*

After what felt like a century, Jeff finally pulled into her driveway. Nicole hurriedly said her good-byes, one foot edging toward the door.

"Nice meeting you," Guy said politely.

"You too," she lied. She felt as if she'd wasted a week with the guy instead of a single boring evening.

Courtney had to get out of the passenger seat to let Nicole exit the car. They faced off in the driveway, barely able to make out each other's features in the dim light from the porch.

"You owe me," Nicole whispered, pointing an index finger at her friend. "You owe me big!"

# Twelve

"Are you sure you feel well enough to go to mass, Mom?" Miguel yelled to her from the sofa. "Maybe you should wait another week."

Mrs. del Rios's voice floated back from the bedroom she shared with Rosa. "I don't *want* to wait, Miguel. I feel fine."

Miguel shifted uncomfortably on the cushions. In a minute his mother and sister would come out to the living room, dressed for church and expecting him to drive them. No one would try to make him attend mass—he was sure of that—but the situation made him uneasy all the same.

Now that his prayers had been answered, did it mean he should go voluntarily?

And what about the promise he'd made God the night he'd snuck into church to light that candle for his mother? He'd said that if God made his mother well, he'd never doubt him again. It seemed an incredibly foolish promise now, one he could never keep. He could control the things he did, but not the things he thought. Could he honestly say he'd never have doubts again? He should have promised something more concrete . . . something he would have been able to deliver.

Even so, he'd made the vow he'd made. Shouldn't he at least *try* to keep it?

He wanted to. The problem was figuring out how. And even if having his prayers answered didn't necessarily mean he had to go back to church, did not having doubts mean he did? It kind of seemed like it might.

He shook his head and groaned. He wasn't *against* going to church. Not anymore, anyway. It was just that he hadn't been for so long—not since his father had died. Miguel imagined the entire place coming to a halt when he walked back through those doors. In his mind, he saw faces staring and fingers pointing. The mere idea was painful to someone who dreaded scenes the way he did. Not to mention confession! He'd have to get poor Father Sebastian to reserve an hour simply to scratch the—

"We're ready!" his mother announced, snapping him out of his trance. "How do we look?"

She and Rosa both did a slow turn in the living room, modeling dresses he'd seen a hundred times. That morning, though, the happiness in their faces made the tired old clothes seem fresh.

"You look beautiful," he answered honestly. "Really beautiful."

His mother seemed to realize he was serious. "Thank you, *mi vida*," she murmured, a flush coming into her cheeks. She looked down at the floor, then at Rosa, then finally back at him. "Well, if you're ready . . . ," she said, almost shyly.

"Oh. Right."

He rose slowly from the couch. His family watched him expectantly.

*They just want a ride, that's all*, he thought, feeling uneasier by the second. *They're not expecting anything from you.*

But it was no good. He was expecting something from himself. And maybe . . . maybe someone else expected something too.

Somehow he managed to swallow. He could feel the blood pulse in his neck and he didn't dare look at their faces as he made his final decision.

"Uh, could you . . . I mean . . . um . . . do you mind waiting a minute?" he faltered. "I want to change into my suit coat."

"I can't believe you're already leaving," Caitlin said sadly, carrying Mary Beth's small suitcase to the door. "It seems like you just got here."

"That's because I did," Mary Beth replied cheerfully.

Jenna felt herself cringe a little. *She doesn't even realize how much Caitlin misses her*, she thought. *Or else she doesn't care.* She shook her head quickly, banishing the disloyal thought.

Even so, it was impossible not to see how eager Mary Beth was to be back on the road to Nashville. The whole family had gone out to breakfast at a favorite restaurant after church to celebrate being together. It should have been fun, but Mary Beth had checked her watch so often that everyone at the table had noticed. Their mother had finally called her on it.

"Are you in a hurry, dear?" she'd asked. "I thought you weren't leaving until one."

"Yeah, probably. But if I get done early and Gail gets done early, I wouldn't mind heading back sooner. It's kind of a long drive—and the later we leave, the worse the traffic will be."

It *was* a long drive, but Jenna couldn't help wondering what Mary Beth thought she had to "get done" before she left. The way she talked, she made visiting sound like a chore.

"Do you have everything?" Mrs. Conrad asked now, bustling into the entry to join them. "Here, I packed you and Gail some sandwiches for your trip."

"Aw, Mom. We just ate lunch, and Gail and I can always stop for a burger or—"

"Take the sandwiches," Mrs. Conrad insisted, forcing the bag on her daughter. "These are better for you."

Mary Beth rolled her eyes, but she took them and gave her mother a hug.

A horn sounded from the street outside.

"That's Gail," Mary Beth said anxiously. "I have to go."

"Tom!" Mrs. Conrad called. "Girls! Your sister is leaving."

Jenna's dad emerged from the garage a moment later, Sarah right behind him. Maggie and Allison ran in from the other direction.

"Well, this is it, then," said Mary Beth, beaming. She hugged everyone. For a minute the family became a tangle of awkward arms and heads bumping into each other. Then the snarl of limbs miraculously divided into eight separate people again, and Mary Beth stood smiling with one hand on the doorknob and the other on her suitcase.

"All right. Take care." She opened the door. A freezing rain was falling outside, and Jenna shivered involuntarily. "Got to dash," Mary Beth said, and she was off, racing through the drizzle to her friend's waiting car.

Everyone crowded into the open doorway, waving until the car pulled away.

Jenna shivered again.

"Close the door!" Maggie said, trying to grab the doorknob from Caitlin, who had somehow ended up in front.

"I will," Caitlin said, still gazing down the street. Slowly, reluctantly, she shut the door. The younger girls scattered—all but Jenna.

"You'll see her again at Christmas," Mrs. Conrad told Caitlin.

"Sure you will. Cheer up, Cat." Mr. Conrad ruffled her brown hair as if she were Sarah. "Could you give me a hand in the garage?" he asked, turning to his wife. "I can't quite get that new shelf up, but if you hold one end while I screw in the other . . ." They wandered off together.

"I can't believe she's already gone," Caitlin whispered to the floor.

Jenna heard the hurt in her sister's voice; she wished Mary Beth were there to hear it too. Caitlin had been so excited to have her favorite sister at home, but Mary Beth had barely noticed. She'd talked to Caitlin, of course, but hadn't paid her any particular attention. If anything, she'd made Maggie her special pet. And instead of accepting Sarah's offered bed, which would have meant sharing a room with Caitlin, Mary Beth had opted for the sofa bed in the den.

"It's bigger," she'd said. "I get so tired of those cramped excuses for beds in the dorms."

She'd changed since she'd been away at college. She'd changed a lot.

"I know you miss her," Jenna said, putting a

protective arm around Caitlin. "But she'll be back pretty soon. And in the meantime you've always got me."

Caitlin brightened a little.

"And Abby," Jenna added. "Don't forget about Abby."

Caitlin's head jerked up, her light brown eyes wide with alarm. "Abby!" she gasped. "Abby's in the garage. And Mom's in the garage. . . . I'd better get out there right now!"

She rushed off, so worried that Jenna could barely keep from blurting out her secret plan on the spot. Instead, she hugged herself happily, biting back the words as her sister disappeared.

*Just wait until tomorrow,* she thought, grinning. *Will she ever be surprised!*


"Bye, Amy. See you soon!" Melanie called, waving as Mrs. Covington's car backed out of the Andrewses' driveway. Her smile was wide and cheerful, and completely fake. Sunday evening had come too quickly.

Of course, having a little kid around twenty-four hours a day hadn't been easy. Amy expected regular meals, for one thing, and she got bored if nothing much was happening. She wanted to talk or play games or go outside or watch TV or do *something* from the moment she got up in the morning until the second she went to bed. And even after that, lying half awake in her little cot, she wanted to be entertained.

"Tell me a story, Melanie," she'd begged sleepily. And Melanie had, making up long rambling tales about a princess named Amy and her magic pony, stories that only a child could have loved and that lasted only until the rhythmic rise and fall of Amy's breathing told Melanie she was asleep.

Now Melanie walked back into her huge, silent house and closed the door behind her. The place seemed twice as empty, twice as lonely as before. The lights were on in the entryway, but the living room was in semidarkness and so was the rest of the downstairs. The faint murmur of a television set carried to her from the den, where her father had retreated the moment Mrs. Covington and Amy were out the door. Melanie stared at her shoes a moment, then slowly climbed the stairs to her bedroom. It felt as if her feet were weighted, as if she had to drag them along beneath her, and she pulled herself up by the banister to make her load seem lighter.

In her bedroom, she took the linens off the guest cot and folded it away. Then she threw herself down on her bed, depressed. What was she going to do with herself for the rest of the night?

*I could work on that term paper, I guess*, she thought,

not moving. Her history teacher, Mrs. Gregor, had assigned Melanie's third-period class the mother of all term papers and it was due on Friday.

Melanie rolled over onto her stomach. *Yeah, right.* Like she was really going to work on that now when she still had a whole week.

After a while she let herself think about her mother, and tears came hot and fast, turning the pale pink of her bedspread into a deeper shade. She wondered if her father was crying downstairs, or if he was already too numb. The holidays were always the worst. Sometimes, on a good day, Melanie could pretend that everything was all right with her life. But not on a holiday. Thanksgiving was a bad one, but Mother's Day and Christmas were even worse. Melanie drew in a deep, shuddering breath. She hated the thought of Christmas, and it was only a few weeks away.

She got up from the bed, not bothering to wipe away her tears as she quietly crossed the hall and let herself into her mother's darkened art studio. The place was silent as a tomb, and the click of the door latch when Melanie closed herself inside seemed louder than a gunshot. She leaned against the door a moment as two more tears rolled slowly down her cheeks. Then she flipped on the lights, blinking in the sudden glare.

She didn't really want to paint, but she wanted the feeling of connection with her mother that painting sometimes gave her. She walked along the back window wall of the studio, seeing only her own sad image reflected in the glass; then, with a sigh, she turned to the built-in flat files and began rummaging for some paper. The paper in the top drawer was plain watercolor stock—various sizes and weights, but all white and just barely textured. She wanted something more interesting, something that would inspire her. She looked further down, then further still. In the bottom drawer was some thick, rough-edged rice paper, full of squiggly fibers. Melanie smiled slightly, remembering her mom's Chinese phase. Mrs. Andrews must have purchased the paper then.

Melanie thumbed carefully through the sheets, thinking it almost a shame to add paint—the paper was practically art already. One sheet had dark, straw-like inclusions; another, bright orange petals . . . *Maybe Mom couldn't bear to mess them up either*, she thought, pulling the drawer open wider.

The sheets got larger toward the bottom of the stack, extending all the way to the back of the drawer, and the final few were the size of posters. Melanie thought of painting something large, something that would take several days, and liked the idea. She tugged at the edge of one of the bottom sheets, but it was snagged on something. She leaned over and peered into the back of the drawer, trying to spot the problem. She tugged again. This time the sheet came forward, but so did all the ones underneath it, dragged along as if weighted. Melanie dropped to her knees and put her hand into the drawer, feeling around at the very back. Her fingers touched something solid—a book? Getting a grip on the edge, she lifted it into the light.

She was so surprised that she sat down hard on the concrete floor, forgetting everything else. The book in her hands was a Bible, a heavy, leatherbound volume with gold on the edges of the pages. She'd probably held a Bible only two or three times in her life. Running light fingers over the crinkly white leather, she traced out the words HOLY BIBLE. What was it doing in her mother's things? Where could it have come from?

Slowly, hesitantly, Melanie opened the cover. The first page bore a handwritten inscription in loopy, old-fashioned writing:

*Presented to Tristyn
on the occasion of her fifteenth birthday
by Grandma and Grandpa Wallace*

Melanie stared at it. Her great-grandparents had died before she was born, but she'd had no idea they were the type of people who'd give someone a Bible. And her mother—had she read it? Why did she hide it?

Forgetting all about painting, Melanie stood up and closed the drawer with her foot. She flipped off the lights and carried the Bible back to her room, intrigued. From the evidence in her hands, she could only assume her great-grandparents had believed in God. Had they gone to church? Had they prayed for their granddaughter's soul?

Melanie shook her head as she entered her room, trying to clear the hundred questions racing through her mind. There was one especially big one, though—one that wouldn't go away. What had happened between her great-grandparents' generation and hers to kill her family's faith?

# Thirteen

The first Monday after the Thanksgiving break, the CCHS cafeteria was jammed. Nicole walked in, then hesitated by the entrance, trying to get her bearings.

*It's not that there's so many extra people*, she decided. *It's just that none of them are holding still.* Everyone was flitting from place to place, comparing notes on the holiday. The overall noise level was so high, it was hard to hear individual sounds. Only the loudest bursts cut through the background—the crash of a dropped tray, the squeal of sudden laughter.

Someone grabbed her from behind, going for her ribs through her heavy sweater. Nicole jumped, screamed, and twisted around, only to discover Courtney, laughing at her.

"There you are," Nicole said sulkily, trying to regain a little dignity. "I've been waiting and waiting for you."

"Nice try, but I saw you walk in." Courtney

glanced around the packed cafeteria. "Wow. I don't know where we're going to sit. Did you bring a lunch, or are you buying?"

"I, uh . . . I'm not very hungry."

Courtney narrowed her eyes. "Aren't you sick of dieting yet?"

Nicole was sick of it, actually. And the more she thought about how little her friends appreciated her efforts, the more sick of it she became. She still couldn't believe that Jesse had called her too skinny—and *meant* it. But ever since he had, she'd been thinking that maybe she could finally ease off. Just a little. It was simply that, well . . . she didn't know where to start.

"I had a big breakfast," she lied.

"Yeah. Whatever." Courtney grabbed her by the sleeve and started pulling. "Come on, then. You can stand in line with me."

They moved to the back of the cafeteria line, too far away from the food to even pick up a tray. "So what did you do yesterday?" Courtney asked as they waited, crawling forward step by step. "Anything?"

"Not really. I thought you were going to call me."

"Sorry. I was going to, but then Jeff came over and—"

"Yeah, yeah," Nicole interrupted, not wanting to hear it. "Don't worry. I know where I rank."

"When you get a boyfriend, you'll understand."

Courtney stretched way out past the people ahead of her and finally managed to snag a tray. "It's not that easy, keeping everybody happy."

Nicole didn't know what to say. Did Courtney honestly believe she was keeping *everybody* happy? She decided to respond to the other part instead.

"Well, when I do get a boyfriend, it'll be no thanks to you and your blind dates. Just in case you're wondering, by the way, I'm never going out with Guy again, so don't even think about asking me."

Nicole was all set for a major battle, but Courtney only shrugged. "That's okay. He doesn't want to see you again either."

*"What?"* Nicole screeched. "What did *I* do?"

Her voice was so loud and full of outrage that people in line turned around to look. Courtney waved a dismissive hand, as if to deflect their attention.

"Who knows?" she said. "I told you the guy was weird. Anyway, you don't like him, so what difference does it make?"

What difference did it make? Only the difference between dumping someone and being dumped.

"But what did he say?" Nicole demanded. "What did he say *exactly*?"

"I don't know. He talked to Jeff, not to me. As far as I can tell, you're too normal for him. I guess Mr. Sunday School thought you were a little spacey, a little wild. He doesn't think you're a serious person."

180

"Not serious!" Nicole exclaimed, wounded. "He was the one who wanted to watch cartoons!"

Courtney shrugged again. "Will you forget it?" They had finally reached the food. Courtney set her tray down on the long silver bars and began loading it up, as if the situation didn't deserve a second thought.

*Forget it?* Nicole thought, following her friend. Courtney might as well have told her to stop breathing. She'd never forget it. Never.

She put one hand to her forehead and massaged a spot near the middle as they inched their way through the line. There wasn't a thing in the world Courtney could have said to make her interested in Guy—except that Guy wasn't interested in her. Now she'd *have* to go out with him again. She'd never rest until she knew Guy took her seriously.

Then she'd dump him.

"Ahhh," Leah groaned, sinking down onto her living room sofa and putting her feet up on the table. Her loaded backpack hit the sofa beside her and bounced onto the floor. After the four days she'd just had off, school that Monday had seemed at least an hour longer than usual—maybe two. And then she'd had to do all that midterm research in the library. . . .

She checked her watch—four-forty-five. Her parents wouldn't be home for a couple of hours.

Exhausted, she picked up the remote and turned on the early news.

The first fifteen minutes were the total waste of time she'd craved: weather, sports, so-called human interest. But then the clock reached the top of the hour and they started with the newsworthy stuff again.

"In local news today," the anchor said, "there are additional developments in the city council budget story."

Leah had relaxed down into the couch, but she sat up straight at the mention of the city council.

"According to a well-placed source," the announcer continued, "members of the council voted last month to approve the use of public funds for road and sewer improvements after being treated to elaborate parties and weekend getaways paid for by the Sonix Corporation. Sonix, a privately held company, recently built its headquarters in an undeveloped area on the outskirts of town. The company was originally told it would have to pay for the private roadway and sewer improvements. The council later reversed itself, however, and declared the improvements public. If the alleged link between gifts to the council members and approval of funds for the project can be proved, it would mean—"

"That they're all toast!" Leah shouted gleefully. "Oh, wow, this is great."

She knew she shouldn't hope the story was true—but she did. With all the accusations flying around, it seemed likely at least some of them were true, and Leah couldn't forgive the council for letting the Junior Explorers down. Besides, the more pressure they were under, the more hope there was that they'd see the error of their ways and come through with some funds for the bus after all.

*More hope still isn't much*, she admitted.

But she couldn't keep the smile off her face as the news anchor went on and on, building a rumor from an unnamed source into a case for the prosecution.

Her fingers crossed. She closed her eyes.

*You never know*, she thought.

"You're here!" Jenna cried, bursting into the garage.

Her father was climbing down from the driver's seat of his van. "I said I would be, didn't I?"

Jenna ran forward and hugged him. "I know. But Mom and Sarah already left, and I was worried you wouldn't be able to get off work early."

Mr. Conrad's smile pulled to one side of his mouth. "It wasn't easy. I thought Ross was going to have an anxiety attack."

Jenna's father was an accountant. A few years before, he and a coworker, Ross Cresswell, had decided to leave the big company they worked for and open their own firm. Jenna still remembered the old days, when her father's hours had been so regular the family could set their watches by them. Now he worked later and later, and sometimes on Saturdays, too.

"What's Ross's problem?" she asked, pulling her father impatiently into the house. "Can't he add up numbers without you?"

Her father stopped walking. "I don't think that's very funny," he said severely, adjusting the knot on his necktie. "How many times have I told you that accountants do more than just add?"

Jenna only laughed. "I know. They subtract, divide, and multiply, too."

"Can't fool you." Her father smiled good-naturedly at the long-standing joke between them. "Just let me change out of these clothes and then we'll get busy."

Jenna paced distractedly while she waited for him to come back. Her plan was a surprise. They had to move fast, before Caitlin got home from work, or they'd be caught right in the middle.

Her father pounded on an upstairs door. "Come on, you girls," he called to Maggie and Allison. "I've got a job for you."

"Aw, Dad!" they whined in unison. Their bedroom door opened a crack. "What?"

"Your sister's cooked up a little plan, and we need your assistance."

Maggie stepped out onto the landing and peered

down at Jenna, who was pacing at the bottom of the stairs.

"Oh, goody," she said. "I can hardly wait."

Allison ventured reluctantly out behind her, her expression showing she fully expected some fate worse than death.

"Oh, for Pete's sake!" Jenna exploded. "We're just going to move some furniture. It'll take ten minutes."

As things turned out, it took a lot longer. Carrying the double bed down the two flights of stairs from Jenna's room to the den was a slow, awkward process, even though they took the mattress, box springs, and frame down one piece at a time. The thick, heavy mattress was hard to keep a grip on, and turning the corners was really a challenge. On top of that, no one could see their feet to tell where they were walking. Going down the stairs blind was more of a thrill than Jenna had counted on, but at last all the pieces were down.

"Gee, only two more to go," Mr. Conrad teased, sucking blood from a knuckle he'd cut on the bed frame.

If anything, moving the twin beds was worse. True, they were lighter, but taking them upstairs meant fighting gravity the whole way.

"Stop pushing!" Maggie whined as they climbed. "I can't go that fast."

"Dad and I are carrying most of the weight,"

Jenna snapped back. "And at least you and Allison can see where you're going. Now hurry up before I drop this."

Jenna's arms were burning and her heart was pounding so hard she felt half dizzy before they made it to the top with the final piece. Then they hurried back downstairs and moved the double bed that used to be Jenna's into Sarah's room, setting it up where the two twin beds had been. Maggie and Allison weaseled off after that, and Jenna and her father went back up to arrange the single beds in Jenna's room.

"It looks awfully tight in here now," Jenna said, experiencing her first brief moment of uncertainty.

"Well, you're obviously not going to have as much room as you did. But if you turn the beds ninety degrees, so their heads are both against that wall, I think it will be a lot better. Then you can put the dresser over there. . . ."

Mr. Conrad began putting his plan into action. Jenna helped, and together they lifted and shoved and coaxed and nudged the furniture into place.

"That looks good," Jenna said at last, relieved. "Now we just have to make up the—"

A brief blast from a car horn sounded in the garage.

"Mom's home!" Jenna exclaimed.

"Run on down and see if she needs a hand," her father said. "I'll put clean sheets on these beds."

186

"Thanks, Dad!"

Jenna flew down the stairs, completely forgetting how tired she had been only minutes before. Bursting into the garage, she nearly collided with her mom and Sarah, who were carrying in bags of groceries. "Did you get it?" she asked excitedly.

"I don't know how I let you talk me into this," Mrs. Conrad replied dubiously, shaking her head. "It's in the car."

"Wait till you see it!" Sarah piped up. "They had every sort of color, but I said we should get . . ."

Sarah's advice was lost as Jenna dashed to the back of the station wagon, too impatient to listen. There were two more bags of groceries at the end of the cargo area, and there, behind the food, was a brand-new, cloth-covered dog bed, the exact same shade of lilac as the drapes in Jenna's room.

"Good job, Sarah!" Jenna exclaimed, pulling it out and holding it up to her nose. It smelled of new fabric and cedar filling. "You picked just right."

The youngest Conrad beamed as Jenna sped by her again, clutching the bed to her chest. She had to finish before Caitlin got home!

Her father was working on the second set of sheets when Jenna crashed back into her room. "Look!" she said triumphantly.

"Where are you going to put that?"

"Good question." She hadn't quite figured that out yet.

Abby was only a medium-sized dog, but the new dog bed was still a good size. And with the two twin beds, the once spacious center of the room was pretty nearly filled. Jenna turned a slow circle, considering her options before deciding on the corner next to the closet. She put the bed down there and plumped it up invitingly. Then she crossed to her desk and retrieved the drawing she'd hidden earlier.

Her artwork was a crayon rendering of a shaggy gray dog with a decidedly hopeful expression on its face. The dog sat on a springlike patch of grass and flowers, the name ABBY printed over its head in pink block letters. Jenna taped the drawing to the wall above the dog bed, then pinned a big purple bow underneath. "There!" she said, happy with her handiwork.

"And *voilà*!" her father added, giving the second bedspread a final tweak. They were finished.

"Now all we have to do is wait for Caitlin," Jenna said, barely able to contain her excitement.

Mr. Conrad checked his watch. "She ought to be here any second."

Sure enough, only a few minutes later Jenna heard the front door opening. She raced down the stairs, her dad, Maggie, and Allison lagging only a few steps behind her. Mrs. Conrad and Sarah came out of the kitchen, and the entire family converged in the entryway. Then, comically, everyone seemed to realize they were going to give the whole thing away and began examining the furniture or the pictures on the wall, trying to look as if they all just happened to be there by accident.

Caitlin stood in the doorway, taking in the unusual sight. Her coat was unzipped, showing her bright work smock underneath, and her normally pale cheeks were flushed pink from her walk home. "What's going on?" she asked nervously.

"Nothing," said Mrs. Conrad.

Caitlin pulled Abby's leash in tighter, until she practically had the dog by the collar. Abby's skinny tail wagged uncertainly, then gradually drooped under the scrutiny.

"I was, uh, just taking Abby to the garage. She wasn't going to be in the house for more than a minute. It, uh . . . it was easier to come in this way, that's all."

"Okay." Mrs. Conrad inspected a picture frame for dust.

Caitlin gave them all one last sideways look, then hustled off toward the garage. The moment the door closed behind Abby's tail, Maggie and Allison burst into giggles.

"Knock it off! Come on, you're going to give the whole thing away," Jenna whispered, motioning for them to be quiet. They stifled themselves, turning red in the face with the effort.

But when Caitlin came out of the garage and walked into the room she had shared with Sarah, even Jenna could barely keep still. Especially when her sister popped back out a moment later, her forehead wrinkled with confusion.

"Okay, you guys—really. What's up? What happened to my bed?"

"What bed?" Sarah asked innocently, keeping the straightest face in the group.

Jenna had planned to make the moment last until Caitlin was completely baffled, but her sister's woeful expression was too much for her. She burst out laughing, and so did everyone else.

"Come on!" Jenna said, grabbing Caitlin's arm and practically dragging her up the stairs. "I want to show you something."

The rest of the family stayed behind as Jenna rushed her sister up to the third-floor room that had once been Caitlin's own. She pushed the door open wide and pulled Caitlin in behind her.

"Surprise!" she cried. "Don't move away, Caitlin. Move in with me!"

Caitlin's mouth opened, then shut, then opened, like a fish left out of water. "I—I—" she stammered. Her brown eyes filled with tears and she slowly shook her head. "I can't," she choked out, barely above a whisper. "I wish I could. But there's Abby . . ."

It was the moment Jenna had been waiting for, the crowning part of her plan. Spinning around, she pointed triumphantly to her special gift, the dog bed she'd paid for with her own money.

"Mom said Abby can stay! And she doesn't have to live in the garage anymore—she can sleep in here with us."

Caitlin stared—first at the lavender dog bed and its fancy purple ribbon, then at Jenna. And then she burst into tears, huge, messy sobs that shook her entire body.

"Caitlin! Caitlin, no!" Jenna cried, distressed. "What's the matter? What did I do? Oh, no, I thought you'd be happy!" She threw her arms around her and hugged her hard, desperately trying to comfort her.

"I am. I am happy," Caitlin sobbed. She raised her soaked face from Jenna's shoulder and swallowed convulsively. "Oh, Jenna . . . thank you."

*She's crying from joy,* Jenna realized, and a moment later, so was she. Tears rolled down their faces as they clung to each other, crying until they laughed. And once they started laughing, they laughed even harder than they'd cried. Big, gasping peals that set Abby barking all the way from the garage.

That night, lying side by side in their beds, Caitlin spoke to her out of the darkness. "Jenna? You awake?" she murmured.

"Yeah. But I thought you were sleeping."

"Nah. Just lying here . . . just drifting." Caitlin hesitated a moment. "You know what I was thinking?"

"What?"

"You remember that movie we saw, the one

where the man and the woman missed each other so much? They couldn't stand to be separated, so they'd call each other when they went to bed, then leave the phone off the hook all night, just to hear each other breathing."

"Um, yeah. I think so." Jenna wasn't sure which movie Caitlin meant, but her description sounded vaguely familiar.

"Well . . . I was thinking," Caitlin said dreamily. "Sometimes, when I pray, it feels like God is all around me—so close that when I'm done I almost hate to say amen. Saying amen—in a way, that's like ending the call . . . like hanging up, you know? It feels like God just evaporates out of the room. So that made me think . . . wouldn't it be great if we could leave a prayer off the hook? Just leave it off the hook forever. Then, whenever we stopped to listen, God would be right there, breathing."

Her sister's idea moved Jenna in a way she couldn't explain. A tear slipped from the corner of one eye and ran down her face to the pillow. She couldn't believe what she'd almost given up just to gain a little privacy.

"I really love you, Cat," she whispered. "Leave a prayer off the hook for me, okay?"

# Fourteen

"So do you have any idea what this is about?" Jesse asked Melanie as he parked his BMW in front of Peter's house.

Melanie shook her head. "I already told you no. Peter was acting totally secretive on the phone."

"Nice of him to assume we don't have anything better to do than come running to random Eight Prime meetings," Jesse grumbled.

Melanie ignored him as she unbuckled her seat belt and let herself out of the car. Jesse was just bent out of shape because Peter had told Melanie to call him instead of calling him directly, and she was far more interested in finding out why Peter was holding an emergency meeting than in listening to Jesse complain. She hurried up the walkway to Peter's front door, not bothering to check if Jesse was following her.

"Come on in!" Peter cried excitedly, pulling the door open before she'd even knocked. "Hey, Jesse, hurry up!"

Everyone else was already sitting in the living

room, and—with the exception of Peter and Jenna—they all looked equally baffled. Melanie assumed they were wondering the same thing she was: Why had Peter called them there that Tuesday night? She hurried to squeeze in beside Leah on the sofa, and Jesse took his usual chair.

"Okay. Are you ready?" Peter asked them, positively bursting. "Everybody, hang on to your hats."

"We're not wearing hats," Nicole said impatiently. "And if you drag this out one more second, I swear I'm going to scream."

Peter smiled, his teeth flashing white. "We got it!" he said triumphantly.

Something froze in the pit of Melanie's stomach. It didn't seem remotely possible, but he could only mean one thing. . . .

"Got what?" Nicole demanded. "I mean it, Peter. Don't be so—"

"It's the money, isn't it?" said Melanie. "We got the money for the Junior Explorers."

Peter nodded. The group went wild.

"What? *How?*" Ben shouted.

"Who cares how?" Nicole cried. She threw her arms over her head, as if she'd just won a race. "Free at last! Oh wow, I can't believe it."

Leah sat forward on the couch. "It's the city council! They can't take the heat anymore, so they thought they'd throw us a bone to help clean up their image."

"Some bone!" Jenna protested. "They're giving us ten thousand dollars!"

"Leah's probably right," Peter said, still smiling. "It's probably a ten-thousand-dollar attempt to buy themselves some decent publicity. But why should we care? As far as I'm concerned, they're just giving us the money they'd already promised."

"Now we can buy that private school bus," Miguel said.

"Let's hurry up and get it," Jesse said. "Did you call that friend of yours yet, Peter?"

"Well, no. I wanted to make sure that's what everyone wants to do first."

"Why wouldn't we?" Jesse demanded.

"I almost wish we wouldn't take their money," Ben said sadly, breaking into the conversation.

"What?" Nicole screeched. "Are you crazy?"

"Yeah, Ben," said Jesse. "What are you talking about?"

"It's just that . . . well, I wish we had earned the whole thing by ourselves. We said we were going to. And it feels like cheating now, taking their money for nothing."

Jesse and Nicole made outraged noises.

Melanie silenced them quickly. "No, you guys. I know exactly what Ben means. It was our project, and now it's like someone else finished it without us."

"Exactly!" Ben said.

"But we shouldn't believe we didn't earn every cent," she continued, "because in a way, we did. If it wasn't for us, no one would even know about the Junior Explorers' bus, and the council would never have come through with that money."

"She's right," Leah said. "Besides, Ben, look at it this way: because of Eight Prime, the kids are going to get a bus that's twice as good."

"That's right," Peter agreed. He looked around the group. "So what's the verdict? Do I call Mr. Haig or not?"

All eyes turned to Ben. He held his ground for a moment, then sighed and reluctantly nodded.

Melanie felt a little twinge, almost as if she had hoped he'd say no, but the instant he moved his head, everyone else jumped in: "Yes! Definitely! Do it right away!"

Peter laughed and held up a cordless phone that had been hidden behind Jenna on the love seat. "If you want, I'll do it right now."

At lunchtime the next day, there was more excitement, but of a far less pleasant sort. At noon, Jenna and Peter had called Mr. Haig from a pay phone to see if he'd talked to the private school yet, and that was when they'd found out that they didn't have enough money. Now everyone crowded into a corner table in the cafeteria to hear the upsetting details.

Peter looked grim. "We've got the twenty thousand dollars for the purchase price, but the school expects us to pay the sales tax, and that's another fourteen hundred dollars. Then Mr. Haig told me we shouldn't drive the bus off the school grounds until we have it insured. My dad's making some calls about insurance today, but expect another big chunk of cash for that, and we'll probably have to pay at least six months' worth in advance."

Jenna had expected the others to be bummed, and they were. Nicole, in particular, looked as if it had just rained all over her Easter bonnet.

"Come on, you guys, it's not that bad," Jenna said, not wanting the group to lose heart. "So we're a little short. We can earn that much in one good event. We can still get that same bus."

"Yeah, if they hold it for us," Leah said. "Did they mention how much longer they'd be willing to wait?"

Jenna glanced at Peter, who squirmed uncomfortably. "Well, apparently they're kind of in a hurry."

"So let's do something fast!" Nicole urged. "This weekend, even."

"I don't mean to be negative," said Miguel, "but I don't know how we could put anything good together that fast. We don't even have an idea, let alone time to act on it."

Nicole scrunched up her face in frustration. Jenna knew how she felt.

"You know, fourteen hundred dollars just isn't that much money," Jesse said reflectively, leaning back on the bench. "It is if you don't have it, but it's not like we're taking cash out of these people's pockets or anything. Why doesn't the school just let us go ahead and pay the taxes and owe them a balance on the bus for a month or two? We're good for it." He turned to Peter. "Probably everyone at your church will vouch for us."

"He's right," Melanie said. "That amount should be nothing to a fancy private school. Why don't you ask them, Peter?"

Peter brightened, and Jenna felt her own spirits rise.

"All right, I will," he said. "It sure can't hurt to ask."

"In the meantime," said Ben, "we ought to be thinking up fund-raisers. We should meet here again tomorrow to talk about how much more money we'll need altogether—with tax and insurance and everything—and find out what the school tells Peter. Then we can figure out how to earn it."

They agreed, some more eagerly than others, before the bell rang for classes. Ben dashed off immediately, anxious to get to gym before the rest of the guys showed up to harass him. Leah and Miguel split for biology, and a moment later Nicole, Melanie, and Jesse left too. Jenna and Peter were the last ones at the table, and pretty close to the last ones in the whole cafeteria.

"I guess we can't put it off any longer," Jenna sighed, wishing she'd had some time alone with Peter. "Want to walk me to choir?"

"In a second." Peter reached into his front pocket. "I have something I want to give you. Here. Hold out your hand."

Jenna extended her hand palm up, expecting him to drop something in it. Instead, he reached forward and quickly tied something soft and bright around her wrist, his fingers fumbling slightly as he made a good square knot.

"It's a friendship bracelet," he explained. "Maura taught the Junior Explorers how to make them, and I made this one for you."

The bracelet was made of blue, purple, and pink embroidery thread knotted so tightly it appeared to be a woven strip of cloth. The colors formed a pattern of repeating chevrons down its flat, narrow length.

"I know it's not much," he said anxiously. "I wish it were something better. Gold or something."

For some reason, the bracelet Jenna had taken

a shine to at Mr. Davin's jewelry shop popped into her head. She could almost see it again—the perfect open heart of the top, the rich golden rope and hand-shaped clasps. At the time, with fantasies of a romance with Miguel filling her head, she'd thought it was the most perfect piece of jewelry she'd ever seen. Now she knew she'd been wrong. The handmade bit of cloth Peter had just tied around her wrist beat it by a mile.

"It's beautiful," she whispered, feeling blood rise in her cheeks. "I love it."

Peter smiled shyly. "Well, maybe it's good enough for now. I used colors I knew you liked. See?"

He rested a finger on the bracelet that circled her wrist. She imagined she could feel his warmth right through to her skin.

"Pink and purple and blue—those are your favorites, right?"

Jenna nodded mutely, afraid to trust her voice. Even if they hadn't been her favorites before, they definitely would be now.

When Leah got home from school that afternoon, another unpleasant surprise was waiting. She unlocked the door of the Rosenthals' small mailbox in the downstairs lobby of their condominium building only to find an ominous-looking, magazine-sized envelope wedged in so tightly she could barely pull it out. It was addressed to Ms. Leah Rosenthal, and her heart sank even before she saw the return address. There was only one thing it could be.

U.S. GIRLS CORPORATION, 1 GIRLS AVENUE, NEW YORK, NEW YORK was emblazoned in red-and-blue-striped letters across the upper left corner of the stark white envelope. Beneath that someone had scrawled in red ink: *Important information enclosed!!! Please respond immediately.*

She took the elevator instead of the stairs, glaring at the hateful thing all the way to the fourth floor. When she finally reached her living room and tore it open, this is what she read:

> *Dear Leah Rosenthal:*
> *Congratulations on being the Missouri winner in the U.S. Girls national modeling search. As you know, hundreds of girls participated in the contest in every state, but we picked you!*

"No. Really?" she muttered sarcastically. "Come on, already. Get to the point."

> *We are now finalizing arrangements for the January finals to be held in Hollywood, California. Gifts and accommodations for you and your three guests will include . . .*

Her eyes scanned listlessly down a long paragraph bristling with words like *beautiful*, *stunning*, and *fabulous*. "Whoopee."

*At this time, participants are required to complete the attached forms, including the biography, guest registry, academic profile, and essay.*

"Essay?" Leah perked up a little. Could there actually be some aspect of the contest that wasn't based strictly on looks?

*It's possible*, she thought as she flipped hurriedly through the packet in search of the essay form. *They're giving out scholarships, aren't they?* They couldn't send illiterates to college.

She was dying to know what the question would be. Maybe something like *If you were the President of the United States, what's the first bill you would sign into law?* Or *What's the single biggest problem facing youth today?* Or it could be something environmental: *What measures must we all take now to assure our planet's future?* Leah liked writing essays—the tougher the better.

At last she found the question: *What does being a U.S. Girl mean to you?*

"Oh, brother," she said, disgusted. "Believe me, you don't want to know."

She carried the paperwork into her bedroom and threw it onto her desk. Despite the red ink on the envelope, the cover letter inside said she had two weeks to complete and return all the forms. That gave her plenty of time. She'd deal with the stupid thing later.

Maybe.

# Fifteen

Melanie found her father in his study after school on Thursday. He was wearing his favorite ratty bathrobe, but the reading glasses barely clinging to his nose and the brisk way he was sorting through the papers on his desk told her he was sober. *Good*, she thought. *Perfect timing*.

She slid into one of the red leather chairs in front of his huge desk. "Hi. What are you doing?" she asked.

"Getting together some of this garbage for taxes. I ought to hire an accountant—it just gets worse every year."

"You can do it, Dad." She didn't point out that he didn't have anything else to do, but they both knew it was true. Mr. Andrews had taken early retirement from his mining company shortly after his wife's death—the better to drink himself into oblivion.

"I know. It's just a major pain in the neck." He

pushed the papers to arm's length across the polished mahogany, as if to get them out of his sight. "So what's new with you? How was school?"

"The same. Listen, Dad, I need to talk to you about Eight Prime. I was wondering if you could maybe help us out."

Her father sat up straighter. "Sure. How?"

She told him the whole story of how they had picked out the perfect bus, how they'd thought they had all the money, and how they'd come up short.

"We'd hoped that the school might let us owe them the difference for a while, just until we can work it off, but Peter's friend talked to them today and they said no way. They're being really hard-nosed about the whole thing, especially considering we didn't even know we had to pay the sales tax. They could have told us that when they told us the price, don't you think?"

"Ah, the government strikes again," Mr. Andrews said sarcastically, nodding toward the papers on his desk. "But I'm afraid it's customary for the buyer to pay the tax. Where do I come in?"

"Well, I was thinking—I mean, I was *hoping*—that maybe you could lend us the difference." She pressed on in a rush, before he could say no. "It would only be for a few weeks. We're so close now, and none of us wants to lose this bus. I'll understand if you don't want to, but I thought we could probably afford it and—"

"Save your breath," her father cut her off. "I'm not going to lend you the money."

Melanie stared, stunned, her last hope dashed. She'd really thought he'd go for it—it wasn't as if she asked for so much.

"I will, however, *give* you the money."

"Wh-What?"

"Sure," he said, smiling. "I'm proud of you, working so hard to help those kids. I'd like to do my part." He had already pulled his checkbook from the drawer and started writing. A moment later he tore a check from the register and held it out. "Here you go."

"Oh, thanks, Dad!" she said, rushing around the desk to hug him before she took the check from his hand. "But, Dad," she protested when she looked at it, "this is too much! You wrote it for two thousand, five hundred dollars."

"Don't thank me, thank Bill Gates," he teased, referring to the fact that back when he was working he'd invested heavily in the stock of a new little company called Microsoft—a move that had helped make him rich.

"Besides," he added, "you're about to find out you're even shorter on cash than you thought. Gasoline, insurance, registration fees, repairs, new windshield wipers, brake fluid—there are a hundred little ways to spend money on a vehicle. My suggestion is to use whatever you need now and save anything that's left over for future bus maintenance. Sooner or later, you're bound to need it."

He was right, she realized. She gave him one last squeeze, then ran out of the room with his check. "I have to call Peter right now!" she shouted back over her shoulder.

She could hear her dad chuckling behind her as she raced to the kitchen phone.

Peter came straight over the minute he got the news. The two of them sat side by side on the sofa in her living room, and Melanie suddenly realized this was the first time they'd been alone together—*truly* alone together—since the homecoming dance. She wondered if he felt as awkward as she did. Silently she held out the check and nodded for him to take it.

He looked it over, smiling, then folded it in half and tucked it into his T-shirt pocket. "This is great, Melanie. I'm going to call Mr. Haig the second I get home. We might even be able to pick up the bus tomorrow."

She nodded, distracted by the line of his jaw, the way his blond bangs were lighter than the rest of his hair. She was pretty sure he and Jenna had something going on now, but it was hard not to feel a little sad about what might have been between them. If he had only been interested . . .

"So are you and Jenna a couple now, or what?" she blurted out.

He reddened, but his smile increased, as if he were happy she had noticed. "Yeah. We kind of decided . . . after homecoming. We're taking things slow for now, but that's the direction we're headed."

Melanie nodded. "I guess you must be pretty happy?"

He laughed. "I couldn't even tell you how happy. I always knew how I felt, but Jenna . . . well . . ."

His face suddenly became serious, as if he'd read some clue in hers. "You're happy for us, right?" he asked anxiously. "I mean, I never thought you—"

"No! Sure I'm happy for you. Absolutely!" She didn't want to hear what he'd never thought about her: that she was the right girl for him . . . that she and he were anything more than friends . . .

*Peter and I never made sense anyway*, she thought. *Not really*. She'd known that from the start. Still, there was a big difference between knowing a thing was unlikely and knowing there was no chance. It was surprising how much that difference hurt.

"You know what?" she asked, eager to change the subject. "I found an old Bible of my mother's this week. I didn't even know she'd had one."

"Really?" he said, interested. "Where was it?"

"In her art studio." Melanie glanced in the direction of her father's study, made sure they were still alone, then lowered her voice anyway. "I think she hid it in there. There's an inscription in front from my great-grandparents. They gave it to her when she was fifteen."

In spite of her recent disappointment, she managed a mischievous smile. "I might even read it. I suppose it can't hurt to find out what it is I don't believe in."

Peter rolled his eyes but took no offense, used to her fooling around. "I guess it's probably a King James version. Right?"

"Huh?"

"What translation is it?"

"What do you mean, what translation? It's a Bible."

"Sure, but all Bibles in English are translations, right? The books it contains weren't written in English."

She'd never thought about it. "The book, you mean," she corrected, sticking to a point she felt sure of.

But Peter shook his head. "Every one of those things that look like chapters—you know, Genesis, Exodus, Revelations—was written separately, then put together much, much later. So the Bible is really a lot of different books, with different authors, too, even though they're all under one cover now."

"Sounds complicated," she said, already wondering if trying to read it was such a good idea.

"Well, the King James version can be kind of tough—that's the reason I asked. A lot of people still love that translation, but the language is so old that sometimes it barely seems like English. There are newer translations in everyday speech, though, and study Bibles that have notes in them to explain the hard places. You might want to start with one of those."

Melanie looked down at her hands twisting restlessly in her lap. "I really wanted to read my mother's. I mean, that was kind of the whole point."

"I understand. And I think it's fantastic. But if you get bogged down, just don't give up, that's all I'm saying. I'd love to help you out, or lend you a study Bible, or . . . just anything. All right?"

Melanie nodded. "All right."

After Peter left, she felt more lost than ever. She wandered sluggishly up to her room. On her nightstand was a stiff paper folder. She picked it up, sitting on the edge of her bed to look at the picture inside.

She and Peter smiled out, dressed in their best for the homecoming dance and looking like an actual couple. He was a good head taller than she, and handsome in his black tuxedo. Her image clung to his possessively, as if they belonged together.

Melanie sighed. Her image was completely deluded. Even then he'd probably been thinking of Jenna.

She rose slowly from the bed and crossed to her walk-in closet. Opening a seldom-used cedar-lined drawer, she slipped the photograph under her clothes, sliding it way to the back. She had planned to frame it, but now . . . now she wouldn't look at it again for a long, long time.

What would be the point?

"Hurry, Peter," Jenna urged as he turned his car up the short road leading to the staff parking lot. "Hurry, I want to get there first."

Peter laughed. "So do I, but I'd prefer not to kill anyone in the process." He glanced in his rearview mirror. "Jesse and Miguel are right behind us. We'll all see it at the same time."

Jenna nearly held her breath with excitement as they rounded the last curve in the road. All of a sudden, there it was! The Junior Explorers' new bus had appeared through a gap in the trees, parked squarely in the center of the otherwise deserted lot in Clearwater Crossing Park.

"I see it! I see it!" Jenna cried, leaning forward in her seat. "It's blue!"

"It sure is. I wonder why Mr. Haig never mentioned that."

"Maybe he didn't think it would matter."

Peter pulled into the lot and stopped his car

without bothering to park between the lines. Jenna jumped out impatiently just as Miguel's and Jesse's cars came to a stop. Suddenly all of Eight Prime was there on the asphalt, with everyone talking at once.

"Oh, how pretty!" cried Melanie and Nicole almost simultaneously.

"Now that's a bus!" Ben shouted proudly.

Miguel and Jesse ran up to inspect the front tires, and Jesse gave one a hard kick. "Lots of tread," he announced.

"Can you open the door?" Leah asked. "Let's see the inside."

Peter shook his head. "Not unless I can find Chris."

Chris and Mr. Haig had gone to pick up the bus together earlier that day. Chris would be the Junior Explorers' designated bus driver, since a person had to be eighteen to get the required license.

"Where *is* Chris?" Jenna wailed. "I thought he was going to be here!"

"Surprise!" Chris's spiky brown head popped up in the window two seats from the front. He'd been hiding, and judging from the expression on his face, he was pleased with his little joke.

"Open this door!" Jenna heard herself shouting. "Chris Hobart, you open up right now!"

Nicole and Leah both pounded on the glass.

A moment later the door flew open—Chris had pulled the inside lever—and everyone swarmed up the stairs.

"Oh, look! Oh, it's so cute," Jenna said, happy tears springing to her eyes.

"Buses aren't cute, they're cool," Ben corrected, wriggling by her in the aisle. He ran to the very last seat and flung himself down into it. "Dibs!"

"Are you joining the Junior Explorers, Ben?" Jesse asked, also squeezing past Jenna to check out the interior.

There were five rows of charcoal gray seats, divided by the center aisle, and one additional bench that stretched all the way across the back of the bus. Ben was sprawled out in that one as though planning to hibernate there for the winter. Jenna kneeled on a front seat to clear the aisle, and soon everyone had crowded in. There were thrilled shouts of approval as the windows were lowered and raised again, the seats were tested for comfort, and the door lever and dash were inspected. The bus was in perfect condition and cleaner than Jenna would have imagined possible. Her heart swelled with pride. They had definitely done a good thing.

It wasn't until they were all back outside, admiring the chrome and powder blue paint, that their plan to honor Kurt Englbehrt was mentioned.

"Just wait until we get Kurt's name painted on

there," Melanie said. "It will look even better then."

"Yeah. How are we going to do that?" Leah asked Peter. "What's it going to look like?"

Everyone started shouting out their ideas. Ben thought Kurt's name ought to be emblazoned across the front of the bus, with wings on either side like the Harley-Davidson logo. Jesse liked that idea, but said it should be on the back. Miguel wondered why it couldn't be both places. Leah voted for something a little more "discreet," and Melanie suggested plain navy blue lettering down both sides. Nicole thought bright pink would be prettier. Peter said they'd have to check prices to find out what they could afford before anyone got too carried away designing a paint job.

And then for a moment they all stood silently, proudly surveying the bus and feeling the magnitude of their accomplishment. Jenna wondered if Kurt was watching, and if he was as happy with it as she was.

At last Nicole spoke up. "Well, I guess this is it, then, right? I guess this is the end of Eight Prime."

Was it only Jenna whose stomach did a swan dive at the sound of those horrible words? No, everyone else looked as stunned as she felt. They all turned to stare at Nicole.

"We did say we were only staying together until

214

we earned the bus," Nicole reminded them awkwardly. "And that looks like a bus to me. . . ."

"We can't just break up!" Jenna protested. "I mean, not like this, at least. Not in a parking lot!"

Leah was quick to come to her aid. "That would be really awful."

"I agree," Peter said. "We ought to have some type of official last event. A party or something."

"How about a picnic?" Ben suggested. "Let's take the new bus somewhere and have a picnic tomorrow."

"It's a little cold for a picnic," Jesse said skeptically.

"We could have a bonfire," said Miguel. "You know, roast hot dogs and marshmallows and things."

"S'mores!" Jenna said, cheering up a bit. S'mores were her all-time favorite.

"Let's have a potluck," Peter said. "We can decide what we want for a menu; then everyone can sign up for something."

He stopped and turned to Chris. "I guess we shouldn't assume that you're free, Chris, or that you won't mind driving us. If you don't want to go, I suppose we could take a few cars."

"No!" Ben nearly shouted. "We *have* to take the bus!"

Chris chuckled. "I don't mind. You're feeding me, right?"

"Right! And Maura too," Jenna said. "You guys don't have to bring anything."

Chris crossed his hands behind his neck. "Maura's busy with her family tomorrow, so you can definitely count me in. One picnic with bus transportation, coming up!"

# Sixteen

"Do you think the guys built a big enough fire?" Nicole asked the other girls sarcastically. "It's singeing my eyebrows."

The picnic site they had chosen was near the otherwise deserted lake; their bonfire blazed in a ring by the shore. December had stripped the last leaves from the trees, and although Nicole complained about the fire, secretly she was glad of it. The leaping flames and glowing sparks were the only cheerful sights in an otherwise cold, gloomy scene. Gray sky, gray sand, and gray water converged into a flat, lifeless landscape, where the only sounds were their own thin voices and the crackling of the hungry blaze.

Leah laughed. "Just keep the table back here, and maybe the plastic won't melt." She was busy setting up the food and a Coleman stove on Nicole's old card table, with help from Jenna and Melanie. The guys had gone off "exploring," bundled in their winter coats.

*This is the last time we'll be using that ratty old table*, Nicole thought, looking forward to seeing the end of it. Maybe she'd give it to Peter, if he wanted it for the Junior Explorers.

*It'll be weird, though, not seeing it anymore, or that rusted-out cash box on top*. She remembered the first time they'd ever used it, for the car wash in the park. She'd thought then that they'd be holding fund-raisers for at least a year. But now, miraculously, they had reached their goal before Christmas.

Nicole moved a little closer to the fire. Even in flannel-lined jeans and a down jacket, she shivered every time she stepped more than a few feet back from the blaze. Only a genius like Ben would have suggested a picnic in December. Why had they even listened?

"It'll be nice to have our weekends to ourselves again," she said, trying to focus on the positive.

"I guess." Melanie was arranging and rearranging the napkins and plastic silverware with gloved hands. "It doesn't really matter to me one way or the other."

*What?* Nicole would have expected Melanie to be even happier than she was about the end of Eight Prime. A girl like Melanie had to have a million other ways to spend her time.

Leah lit the stove, put a covered pot of chili on to heat, and gazed out over the water. "It's going to seem strange not thinking about the bus anymore, though, or having meetings and events. I'm not sure I'll know what to do with myself."

"Well, you could start by sleeping in," Nicole told her. "That's what I'm going to do. And go to the mall. And . . . well . . . lots of things." For some reason, though, she couldn't think of any just then. There had to be tons of stuff she wanted to do now that she was free again. What had she done before?

"I'll probably start helping Peter with the Junior Explorers every Saturday," Jenna said shyly.

It had spread through the bus like wildfire on the drive to the lake that she and Peter were a couple now, although there had been far too few details to satisfy Nicole. She wasn't even sure who had started the rumor. Those two *had* been sitting awfully close together, though, and there'd been a whole lot of whispering between them. Nicole sighed, knowing that either way they'd be fine. Jenna and Peter didn't need Eight Prime.

*None of us* needs *it*, she told herself, surprised by the thought. So why wasn't everybody happier? Why wasn't *she* happier? The only person who had seemed excited was Courtney.

"Are you kidding me?" she'd screeched when Nicole had called her the night before. "You guys are breaking up? The God Squad is really dead?"

"Yep. Long live the God Squad," Nicole had responded jokingly. It hadn't felt like a death at the time, but it was starting to now.

All those weekends Nicole had been looking forward to suddenly stretched out in front of her—empty. Oh, sure, she'd do stuff. She'd hang around the mall with Courtney and listen to endless Jeff stories; she'd catch up on months-old fashion magazines; she'd go out on more dead-end dates with losers like Guy.

Nicole winced at the thought. That Guy thing was a real thorn in her side.


"Are you sure you guys know where you're going?" Jesse asked for probably the third time. "If we're lost, you can tell me. I can handle it."

Chris and Peter only laughed.

"You've got to be kidding," Chris said. "Two local boys like us lose the California kid? It's just to the top of this bluff."

"That's what you said the last time," Jesse grumbled. Not that Missouri topography was exactly rugged. Even the so-called mountains of the Ozarks were only little bumps compared to the foothills of California. It was just that he was hungry for those hot dogs they were supposed to roast, and trudging through the winter woods was losing what little appeal it had. Miguel and Ben had had the right idea—halfway into their journey the two of them had opted to head back and help the girls.

At last they broke out over the top of a rise and stood on a flat, narrow ridge. Behind them, the ground they'd just climbed sloped gradually, but in front of them it dropped off forty feet. They had climbed higher than Jesse had realized. Below them lay one crooked arm of the lake, its cold gray fingers stretching in all directions. Jesse could barely make out the rock everyone swam from in the summer and the little speck of the bonfire at the end of the main beach.

"Wow," he said. "I didn't realize the lake was so big."

Peter and Chris walked to the cliff and sat on a big flat rock that jutted out over the edge, letting their booted feet dangle in space. It seemed dangerous to Jesse, but he didn't want to look like a coward, so he joined them. The surface of the rock felt like ice through his jeans. Peter and Chris didn't seem to notice, though, and Jesse bit back his complaint, tired of jokes about his California blood.

"I can't believe we're just goofing off today," he said instead. "I can't remember the last Saturday I didn't have something I had to do."

"Are you still helping that man with his yard?" Peter asked.

Jesse groaned. "You mean Charlie? Yeah. I still owe him twenty hours."

"Who's Charlie?" Chris wanted to know.

Jesse liked Chris, so he took the time to explain about Charlie—all except the part about why he was helping him.

"He's a pretty nice old guy, I guess," he concluded. "I don't really understand why he ended up alone, but it might be something to do with the booze. Hard to believe, as frail as he is, but he claims he was an alcoholic."

"Well, alcohol will do some bad things to your body if you don't know when to stop," Chris said. "Maybe that's part of why he's so frail."

"Yeah. Maybe. But he says he hasn't touched a drink in fifteen years."

"Wow." Chris looked impressed. "That's a long time. I guess I can see giving it up like that, though. I can *now*, I mean—I haven't exactly been the king of good behavior myself." He laughed, and Peter joined in with a chuckle.

"What are you talking about?" Jesse asked.

Chris leaned back on his elbows. "Before I met Maura, I was pretty lost. I used to drink all the time, take drugs—you name it. I thought being half conscious was making my life easier. The funny thing is, though, it's actually easier now that I've put all that behind me."

He smiled sheepishly. "When you're in the middle of it, you don't realize how draining it is— sneaking around all the time, breaking the law, lying to everyone. . . . I can tell you, I don't miss it. I don't know if I'll drink again when I turn twenty-one or not, but if I do, it sure won't be like last time. It's nuts to let a substance control you like that."

Chris's words were so similar to Charlie's that Jesse couldn't ignore them. He supposed in a way it would be easier to give up drinking, at least until after high school. It would be a relief not to have to sneak around anymore, not to worry about the coach finding out and kicking him off the team for good. He'd be the man of his word the coach already thought he was.

But if Chris had replaced his addictions with Maura, what could Jesse replace his with? Football was over. That was already one hole in his life. And now Eight Prime was over too—another empty place.

He *could* give up drinking . . . but what else was there?

"Ugh, I shouldn't have had that last s'more," Jenna groaned, following Ben on the trail. "Not after those two chili dogs."

"You should have had s'less," Ben quipped. His humor hadn't changed, but the glance he threw her over his shoulder was positively mournful. He looked ready to cry any minute.

Jenna had noticed during lunch how upset he was. He'd sat half hunched over on a split-log bench like the rest of them, but while everyone else complained about the cold seats and hurried to eat their warm food, Ben's lunch had moved from one side of his plate to the other with very little disappearing. He'd been so subdued, he hadn't even spilled anything. By the end of the meal Jenna had been worried enough to ask him to walk with her along the edge of the lake, to work off the food he'd supposedly eaten.

They were far away from the others now. When the path widened into a gravelly little clearing at the water's edge, Jenna stopped walking abruptly.

"Are you okay?" she asked. "I mean, is anything wrong?"

Ben shook his head rapidly. "No!" His voice came out as a squeak. "What makes you say that?" Traces of tears glistened in his brown eyes.

"I don't know. You just seem a little upset, maybe."

"I'm not upset!" he said quickly.

She looked at him questioningly, inviting him to tell the truth.

"Well, okay. Maybe I am," he admitted miserably. "But I didn't want anyone to know."

"But, Ben, what's the matter? Didn't you think we'd want to help you?"

He was really blinking hard now. He hung his head and one lone tear dropped straight down to the ground.

"I just . . . wish the group wasn't breaking up,

that's all. I know everybody wants to, though. . . . I *hate* it that I'm such a baby!"

Jenna moved to his side and put a comforting arm around him. Strangely, the moment didn't feel nearly as awkward as it could have. "I don't think you're a baby, Ben."

"You don't?" He sniffed—a big, blubbery inhalation.

"No. Actually, I wish we weren't breaking up too."

"Really?" His eyes were big and grateful. He sniffed one last time and gestured to his wet face. "Don't tell the others, okay? I don't want them to think I'm soft."

"I won't." She patted his shoulder. "It'll be our secret."


"So, I guess this is it," Miguel said. From the rock he and Leah had climbed up on, they had a clear view of the picnic site and the powder blue bus in the unpaved parking lot. The fire on the beach was dying down, the sky was beginning to darken, and soon they'd be leaving for home. "Eight Prime's last event, and it's almost over."

Leah snuggled in close to his side and shivered against the growing cold. "It feels weird, doesn't it?"

"Really weird. I don't know what I'll do with myself."

"You know what I was thinking? I was thinking

225

maybe you and I could volunteer somewhere else. Just to keep it going, you know? Maybe even at the hospital. Have you given any more thought to the doctor idea?"

*Me, a doctor!* he thought, still somewhat awed by the prospect. It was probably the biggest dream he'd ever allowed himself—so big he wasn't sure he had what it took to see it through.

*I know I'm smart enough, though. And I'm not afraid of hard work. Besides, if I were a doctor, I'd be able to take care of my family in every way—not just financially. And I could help a whole lot of other people, too.*

"Yes. I think I'm going to do it," he said calmly, amazed by his own boldness. "Maybe we *could* volunteer in the hospital, now that Eight Prime's breaking up."

He frowned a bit at his own words. Breaking up sounded so final. He turned to look at Leah and saw the same torn expression on her face he knew was on his own. They were thinking the same thing: if it hadn't been for pledging to earn the bus with Eight Prime, they wouldn't be together.

Things at the beginning of their relationship had been pretty rocky. It was only their commitment to the group that had kept them around each other long enough to fall in love. Losing Eight Prime was like losing their life preserver. He didn't think they'd need it anymore, but still . . .

"It's sad, isn't it?" he asked huskily.

"Real sad," she answered with tears in her eyes.


"Where's Chris?" Melanie asked Peter.

They had packed up the last things, and despite the bitter cold of evening, everyone was dawdling around the embers of the bonfire, pretending to look for items that might have been missed.

"He's up in the parking lot, warming up the bus."

"Oh." It was really over, then. Any minute they'd all climb into the bus for the very last time and Chris would take them home.

Melanie looked around at the unlikely group of people who'd become her friends—her best friends, really—and tried to imagine saying good-bye. She knew she'd still see them around. She'd see them at school, or maybe she'd run into one of them at the mall or someplace. But it wouldn't be the same.

They'd all gathered in close to the coals now, abandoning even the pretense of a search. They made a tight, silent ring, the eight of them. Eight Prime. A group that, like a prime number, could only be divided by itself.

"You know," Melanie blurted out, "that bus is going to be expensive to keep running. My dad said it's going to need brake fluid, and gas, and wiper blades, and, oh . . . lots of things."

She dared to look up in the silence that followed,

and her eyes locked with Jesse's across the dying flames. Something passed between them, something more like a conspiracy than a truce.

"Tires," he said loudly. "Sure, they're in good shape now, but tires for that baby are going to cost a fortune. Not to mention mechanical stuff. Even if it doesn't break down, what about tune-ups?"

Everyone else suddenly looked up too. There was the beginning of something in all their eyes. . . .

"Antifreeze!" Jenna contributed joyfully.

"Oil changes!" shouted Ben.

"Are you guys saying what I think you're saying?" Peter asked in happy disbelief.

Leah and Miguel exchanged a quick, meaningful glance.

"Brake pads," said Miguel. "Wheel realignments. Armor All and Turtle Wax."

"Don't forget about insurance," Leah added.

"That's right!" Ben leapt in again. "Insurance is going to cost a lot!"

Everyone was smiling now; everyone was excited. And then Melanie looked at Nicole. There was a strange lack of expression in those big turquoise eyes. Nicole's face was completely blank.

*Uh-oh*, Melanie thought. Nicole had always been the least enthusiastic about the group. Was she going to bail out on them now?

*We could still go on without her.* It wasn't as if Melanie's heart would break. Nicole had never really liked her anyway, and she hadn't much liked Nicole. . . .

But then again, hadn't they gotten past that? She'd been there for Nicole at the U.S. Girls contest, and lately they'd gotten along pretty well. They could probably even be friends, if they gave it a chance.

*I would miss her*, Melanie realized. She looked around the circle of familiar faces. *I'd miss them all, even Jesse.*

Eight Prime wouldn't be the same with seven.

"How about it, Nicole?" Melanie asked. "Can't you think of something the bus will need?"

Nicole blinked as if snapping out of a trance. She looked questioningly at Melanie, then turned her gaze on them all. "I . . . uh . . . ," she stammered.

Melanie's heart sank.

Nicole drew in a deep breath and burst out with her thought in a rush. "What about painting Kurt's name, huh? No one's mentioned that, and I'll bet it's going to cost plenty. And I don't want some tiny little lettering, either. It should be big and beautiful and—"

"Expensive!" Melanie cried.

"Money's no object!" yelled Ben.

The smile on Peter's face had been growing word by word. "You know, the Junior Explorers could use a few other things for camp, too."

"The children's ward at the hospital needs

picture books and toys," Miguel blurted out of the blue.

Everyone turned to stare, partially because Miguel rarely offered ideas, but mostly because he'd just opened a door the rest of them hadn't yet seen. Why limit themselves to helping the Junior Explorers when they could be helping others as well?

Jenna's hand jerked up, as if she were in school. "Caitlin said the animal shelter needs donations and volunteers to take care of abandoned animals."

"This old guy I'm helping . . . Charlie . . . ," Jesse said slowly, "his house needs to be painted something awful. He'll never get it done on his own."

"We could do it!" Ben said, hopping from foot to foot in his excitement. "We could do it all!"

"We could," Melanie echoed. "That, and even more."

Peter's eyes scanned the tight little circle; then he stretched out a hand in front of him, palm down toward the dying fire. "What do you say?" he asked them. "Do you want to keep the faith?"

Without hesitation, Jenna put her hand over his. Ben's slapped down hard on hers. "I do," they both said.

Melanie's hand went on top of Ben's. Then came Leah's, Miguel's, Nicole's, and finally Jesse's. Their hands made a stack in the center of the circle—a new pact. Another new beginning.

"Go, Eight Prime," Melanie prompted, forcing the

words past the lump in her throat. "On three . . . One, two, three."

"Go, *Eight Prime!*" they all roared, throwing their hands up into the air. And then came hugs and laughter, and even a few tears.

Eight Prime was staying together.

**Find out what happens next in Clearwater Crossing #7, *New Beginnings*.**

## About the Author

Laura Peyton Roberts holds an M.A. in English from San Diego State University. A native Californian, she lives with her husband in San Diego.